TO LIFE

LIFE

Justine Orme

Justine Orme

Cover Photo: Eric Ward (Unsplash.com)

Cover Design: Colleen Kaluza

Co-Published by: WordWyze.nz

Printed in New Zealand by YourBooks.co.nz

A catalogue record for this book is available
from the National Library of New Zealand

Printed Soft-cover edition: ISBN 978-0-473-48009-7

Epub Edition: ISBN 978-0-473-48010-3

For Frank

Frank, you were the final catalyst that forced me to forget my reservations and put my life on paper.

Growing up with rejection by whatever cause, never feeling completely accepted and wanted, led you into considerable pain. But your faith in our Lord shone. You didn't know how much you were loved. Now you do.

Jesus warned us that we would have trials and tribulations in this world and Frank had more than his share. Through it all, he persevered until his humanity could not handle any more.

Your agony of heart that was never healed on this earth is finally answered in full, and I know you are safe in Jesus.

20 November 2018

My Lord and my God.
I bow before you
and acknowledge
You are King.
You are Lord;
You are God.
Without you,
I would not have lived;
I would not be
the person I am today.
My healer, My Redeemer.

ACKNOWLEDGEMENTS

This has been the hardest thing I have ever had to write. Without my team of prayer warriors behind me, yelling their support, I could not have finished this book. For many of them, the journey has also been personal, and I bow my head to you, for this has not been easy for you, either.

Jenny, Judith, Carley, Sarina, Helen, Liz, Joan and Amanda. I honour you before Heaven for your constant love and encouragement.

There was needed research for the medical side. I was assisted by four people in this.

Janet Huddleston, retired Senior Regulatory Compliance Engineer for Fisher & Paykel Health Care, whose knowledge of the equipment used in the ICU units was brilliant. She gave such detailed explanations of how it was all used, the noises it made, and of course the correct names. Without this, the story would lack depth. Thank you.

Marni Adlam - Thank you for sharing your knowledge and understanding of ambulance and paramedic processes, and the procedures of police attending suicide scenes.

Tom Tate - Advanced Practice Registered Nurse, Certified Registered Nurse Anesthetist - for your valuable information on intubation and the recall of patients after an induced coma.

Stacey Orme. Yes, I know you are my daughter, and I know you keep saying "Mum, I'm a pediatric nurse, not emergency or ICU," however, your research and tireless patience in listening to me and helping me sort all the medical terminology out, so it is correct, is fantastic. You are awesome.

Colleen Kaluza. What would I do without you? Not just my editor, co-publisher and cover designer. But friend, shoulder, prayer buddy.

For all the many, many, women and men who have unstintingly opened their hearts to me about their own experiences with depression and sexual abuse. Thank you. How I wish we had never had to have these conversations.

And of course, **my husband, Stan**. God knew exactly what He was doing when he put us together all those many years ago. You have been my strong tower, my strong right arm. You have loved me through tremendous storms, as I have fought my way to freedom from this horrendous thing. With all my heart, Darling, I love you.

These acknowledgements would not be complete without thanking Xenus and Jules. Whenever I sit down to write, I ask the Lord God to write these words, because I just can't. One day, something different happened. In walked two angels. One was very studious, and the other was a riot of joy. Both were garbed in ancient Roman senate style clothing. I knew they were both scholars. Xenus (pronounced Kainus), wore the Roman senate clothing, which was bordered in red. He was quite a solemn angel and stood behind me, assisting in the writing of this book. Jules was younger and dressed in a shorter toga style, that was bordered in blue, which I can only describe as being a brilliant topaz blue. He was very inquisitive about our world and one day while out for coffee with friends, he made his presence known by looking at everything in the store. Because he brought joy, I just started laughing, randomly for no reason. Such a funny angel.

I'm so grateful for these two angels, Lord. Thank you for sending them.

"I will give you
the treasures of darkness,
riches stored
in secret places,
so that you may know
that I am the LORD,
the God of Israel,
who summons you
by name."

Isaiah 45:3 NIV

WHAT OTHERS ARE SAYING

Judith MacDonald (New Zealand):

This is an amazing book. An exceptional author. It shows the love of the Lord Jesus Christ and his healing power. It's the true story that can heal. Especially for those that feel they are not worthy because of those things that happened to bring them into captivity. The book shows our God is forever with us. It is a heartfelt true story that ends in victory. You won't want to put it down, as it is so captivating as it leads you forward, finally to see the victory.

Pastor Amanda Ford (Matthew Ford Ministries - www.mattford.org):

Justine's grasp on the psychological prison an abused victim faces, is demonstrated perfectly with clarity and simplicity, giving the reader multi-faceted revelation of the issues at play in child sex abuse, both from a natural and spiritual perspective. Melissa's story is one of hope for all, which allows the reader to see that the only path to lasting freedom in any situation is through Jesus Christ and Him alone.

Wendy Queen (Austin, Texas, USA) From Sonzofthunder Prayer Ministries

A wonder! So vital. This beautiful story will set so many free. Not many have addressed this topic. I believe the Lord is really opening these very needed doors and gates for transformation for all. I am honoured to be part of this Kingdom building.

Sarina Ballard (Australia):

Thank you, Justine, for your honesty and your transparency. Justine has put herself in a vulnerable place writing this book, but I believe this book will be a great resource to those who read it. It will bring hope, healing, a renewed faith and restoration. For those of you who would like to experience a freedom that will allow your heart and mind to walk in healing, hope and peace, I would highly recommend this book.

Kathy Simmonds (England):

Having had the privilege to read parts of this book whilst Justine was writing it, I can honestly say it will impact your life! As it has mine. LOVE pours out of every page. The LOVE that the Time Weaver has for each and every one of us, and yes, that includes YOU.

As you read Melissa's story, may you find yourself on your own journey with the Time Weaver.

William J Davey, Q.S.M. (Warkworth, New Zealand):

Let not your heart be troubled, neither let it be afraid - John 14 v 27

The title of this book, *25 To Life*, conjures for me thoughts of a terrible punishment that was unwarranted. For many, this appears to have no end.

I know only too well, the pain suffered by many victims of abuse. When serving in the New Zealand Police, I worked with parents and teachers who were trying to help young people avoid becoming abuse victims. Sadly, this had to include members from within their own families. On speaking one evening with an adult community group, an elderly lady came up to me after the talk, questions and answers, were over with. She whispered to me, "There's nothing new, you know." My heart broke for her. This was probably the first time that she had felt free to voice that pain which had dragged along behind her, in her very long life.

I have always been concerned for those who endure a secret, physical, emotionally crippling pain, enveloped by shame and embarrassment, none of which they deserved.

Justine's book shows there is a way to liberation from these abhorrent acts.

Ian W Johnson (New Zealand) of His Amazing Glory Ministries www.hagmian.com:

As a man and a Pastor, I have had to engage in conversation and counsel regarding the aftermath of sexual abuse, in far too many women and children. This breaks my heart and should never happen. The brokenness and patterns of behaviour that are common to sexual abuse victims are often judged in our society, while the perpetrators hide in a shadowy world of control and manipulation. These men can appear model citizens and escape the public humiliation that manifests through the years in the victim's life. Sexual abuse is the hidden pain carried in the heart of countless women. From my point of view, men need to own their lack of honour toward the beauty that is Woman and let their voices rise to stamp this leprosy out, so women can arise and enter their God-given destiny.

Ian W Johnson is also the author of several books, including:

What Is Mankind?
21 Days Into the Heart of Jesus
His Total Provision
Glory to Glory
Heaven's Sons Reveal on Earth

Helen Macmillan B.Ed. (retired) Co-Leader of *Jewels Alive* , Poet, Psalmist:

This latest book *'25 To Life'*, by Justine Orme, sends you on a roller-coaster of emotions. From shock and horror to renewed hope and joy ... you are gripped by the characters in a "can't put down" story, that brings final redemption to all involved.

Time Weaver is the perfect potter to mould and restore all things.

Justine writes with great power and sensitivity about the very personal and painful subject of child abuse.

This is a story that portrays how light can be restored again after the darkness has come in.

I highly recommend this book, which is written by a talented and visionary woman of God.

Yvonne Marotz (Michigan, USA) of The Arrowhead-LGA Ministries:

Justine Orme sent me a copy of her book, *25 To Life* as she knew it would help the women I work with, in the prisons. So many of them have been sexually abused, and as a result, acted out in various destructive behaviours, which resulted in their being incarcerated.

As I began to read the book, even in the first few pages, I could 'feel' the stirring, the pain that she as a little girl had gone through. I knew this book would hit the spot for these women, and they would identify with the situations as they take place. I know that as Justine 'embraced' the pain and memories, that were a part of her healing, I 'felt' these sensations with her. I know the women will experience this with us both, as they allow the Lord Jesus Christ to heal them also.

I recommend this book for those helping someone to recover from sexual abuse, or for the abused.

There is hope.

Contents

JUSTINE'S FOREWORD

Why 25 TO Life? And why are the chapters numbered back to front?

25 To Life was conceived from my own journey and that of many others. The title is a play on words.

A sex abuse victim or survivor is subject to a life sentence. The sentence the abuser should have received. It's for life. Period.

When Melissa starts her journey, we are onlookers to extraordinary pain. The pain brought on by predators of the worst kind.

For 25 hours, we follow James and Melissa as they journey towards Time Weaver.

This is not meant to be a look into the psychology of abuse. The only way through the miasma of this treacherous, sucking, muddy life, is to keep our eyes directly on Jesus. In all my pain, my suicidal thoughts, anger and the screaming inside me that just never stopped, there is only one place to find peace - in Him.

It never ceases to astound me, the intricacy of the dance that Father God brings us through; the tiny pieces all coming together, that without even one small piece, the puzzle would be incomplete.

25 TO LIFE is my story mixed with many other stories. All have the same foundation, that of being abused as a child.

Yes, Melissa is me, and yes what Ken and Grandpops did is real, but it was not my suicide. Sadly, suicide following on from the depression of child sex abuse is all too common, and my own journey took me down that road. It was only Jesus who stopped me, only the sheer grit to keep going and refusing to give in to that dark bottomless pit of despair. My husband calls it being stubborn. In this case, stubborn works.

There are various scenes I have written into the story that are mine and were my privilege to experience. Time Weaver is, of course, Jesus.

You will notice that the font is a little bigger than is customarily used in a book. This is deliberate, for many of my readers have commented that the larger font in my other books was so helpful. Not everyone is young with good eyesight.

Justine

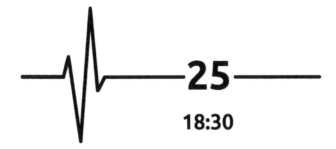

25

18:30

James checked his watch as he waited for the garage door to go up. 6:30 pm on Friday. *Thank God, it's Friday,* he thought. A little bit late home but not so that Mel would worry. Traffic on Friday nights was always abysmal. He was relieved to see her car was already in the garage. *Hopefully, she will be in a better mood tonight,* he thought as he parked the car next to Mel's. What a tiff they'd had this morning, ending with James storming out of the house and going to work, without saying goodbye. Everything ended in a fight. It was as though Mel was blaming him for her junk, as she battled the monsters from her past.

He leaned his head on his hands on the steering wheel.

He hadn't known about *IT* when they married. She hadn't told him. Just a year ago, she had changed. Something had changed, and he couldn't figure it out.

The memories thrashed around in his head, pouring unutterable scenes over and over again through the movie screen of his mind.

What sort of sicko would do that to a child? He wondered. *I love Melissa, I really do, but I can't handle this anymore. Oh, stop being so selfish, James!* he tried to reason with himself. *She is trying. She can't help what the creep did.*

Groaning out loud, he sat up straight and reached for the garage remote to shut the door. He grabbed his stuff and got out of the car. It sounded really quiet in the house. The kids were probably watching TV. *Maybe tonight will be different? Maybe tonight she wouldn't reject his love? She'd never felt abandoned to him in their lovemaking. There was always a wall. She was reserved; shut him out of a part of her he could never reach.* He sighed. *Yes, she will be better tonight, after her counselling today.* James assured himself. *The counsellor will have been able to settle her a bit. Maybe we can have a night of peace, without rehashing over and over again the filth and utter depravity of what was done to her, and to the myriad of the new friends she had made. Why couldn't she just forget about it and move on?!*

Their relationship had deteriorated since Melissa had come out about the sexual abuse she had been subjected to as a young child. All their friends had faced the full-on story. Told over and over and over to anyone who would listen. Many of them had distanced themselves. They couldn't handle the raw pain. "Neither can I," James muttered. If only she would get through this. If only, if only. So many "if only's".

Opening the door from the garage to the house, the first thing that he saw, was nothing. There were no lights on. No dinner cooking. He couldn't hear the kids. Puzzled, James stopped, stepped back into the garage and just checked again. Yes, Melissa's car was there. What? Where was she? Where were the kids? The cat wound himself around James' legs, meowing his hungry cry. "Hello, Puss, where is everyone? Nobody fed you, boy?"

"Mel!" he walked into the kitchen and flicked the light on. "Mel, hello! Honey, where are you?" Putting his stuff on the kitchen counter, he noticed an empty whisky bottle. *Ha! She had a party without me!*

Bounding up the stairs to their room, calling "Melissa! Mel!"

Oh no. She's been at therapy again. Why couldn't she, just ONCE after therapy, actually feel better. Just ONCE. His thoughts tumbled around, seeking answers. Surely her shrink should be able to talk some sense into her by now.

Their bedroom door was shut. Oh, that's the answer. The kids must be at their friends' houses, and Mel has fallen asleep, exhausted after her counselling session. He felt relief at understanding why the house had been in darkness. He turned his bedside lamp on. Melissa was sprawled on her side of the bed. She's so beautiful to me. She looks so vulnerable, just lying there. He leaned over and kissed her. All the past and present of his love for her, in that one gesture. "Honey, wake up. I'm home. If you are too tired to cook, shall I get take-out tonight?" Stroking the beloved face, the tormented look absent in her sleep. She didn't stir. "Mel, wake up, Love."

That's odd, he thought. She usually didn't sleep well. But she was sound asleep this time. He stroked her arm, shaking her gently, and as he did so, noticed a note on the bed next to Mel. He picked it up, expecting to read that she was tired. Let her sleep. The kids were next door. His eyes flickered, line to line, horror dawning on him.

'I'm sorry, James. I can't cope anymore.
I love you so much and know that I am
destroying you.
I am destroying the kids.
It is better this way. Better that I leave.
I love you always.
Tell the children I especially love them.
Always in my heart.
Mel xxxx'

And then he spotted the empty bottle. Her sleeping pills. What?

Stupidly he just stared at the bottle.

"MEL. NO!" He shook her hard. "Mel, wake up!" with no response. "Somebody, help! Help me!!" he screamed to the silent house.

Grabbing at the cordless phone, hands shaking, James dialled emergency.

"What service do you require?" the voice came through the phone.

"Help me! Help me! Please! I can't wake my wife!" His voice wouldn't work. He couldn't make his voice loud enough. Oh God! "I think she's taken all her sleeping pills. She…" Stuttering in distress. "She won't wake up!" James' voice was a thin reed of sound, as he tried to scream his desperation at the dispatcher.

"Sir, is your wife conscious?"

"C...conscious? No. I can't wake her! Mel, wake up. Please, please wake up!" James was shaking her, panicking.

"Is she breathing? What is your name, sir?" The voice came back through the phone. "Sir, give me your address. Stay on the phone with me."

"Ahh, 2 Queens Avenue in B...Bellfield." Stuttering in his panic. "Oh, God. Please hurry." James shook Melissa again while talking to the dispatcher.

"Emergency services are on their way. Stay on the line with me and go and make sure the front door is open and the lights are on. I'm waiting with you until they arrive."

He ran down the stairs, yanked open the front door, flicking lights on everywhere and ran back up to Melissa.

"Sir, the ambulance is just a few minutes away now. Has your wife regained consciousness?"

"No, she won't wake up, I can't wake her! What do I do? She's taken all her sleeping pills after a whisky binge. Oh, God. What do I do?! Why are they taking so long? Please hurry." sobbing, dropping to his knees by the bedside.

"Sir, the ambulance has arrived at your home. You will hear them shortly. Call to them so they can follow your voice. I will stay on the line until they are with you."

"Thank you. Yes, I hear them coming." James yelled as loudly as he could "Up here, up the stairs. Please hurry. She won't wake up." Voice breaking, gasping for air, as howls of anguish broke from him.

The voice on the phone said, "The paramedics are with you now. I will let you go and deal with it. All the best, sir." And the line to hope and help went dead.

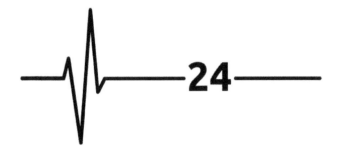

24

Two paramedics. Angels of life. One went to Melissa, and the other smiled at James, as she went straight to work. Reassuring presences edging hope into his confused dread. One led James away from Mel, over to the seat in the corner of the bedroom.

Measured tread, measured voices, calm, reassuring. "How long has she been unconscious?" The second paramedic talked to James.

"I don't know. I just got home from work and found her like this."

Picking the pill bottle up, the paramedic asked, "Do you know how many tablets she had left?"

"No. She gets her prescription once a month. She was taking antidepressants as well, and she drank the rest of the whiskey."

"Would you get all her medication for me, please?"

As James went to their bathroom, one of the paramedics messaged back to base: "drug and alcohol overdose. Female, 40, unresponsive. History of anti-depressants."

"Melissa, open your eyes, Melissa. Can you hear me? Open your eyes. Tell me your name."

James looked eagerly for any response from his wife. Did her eyelids flutter?

"Squeeze my hands, Melissa."

He watched as the paramedics checked her over. Respiratory rate, heart. One put an IV line into her arm with the bag of fluids, while the other attached ECG dots and leads to her chest, hooking her to the monitor. Oxygen mask over her face, the whisper of air being forced into her lungs and the hiss as the air escaped through the small holes, preventing the carbon dioxide being re-breathed. Wiping his face, surprised to find he had been crying, he wondered where the kids were.

"James." A different voice spoke to him.

He turned to see two police standing by him. Confused, he struggled to understand what was happening. "What? What is happening? Why are you here? Do you...you don't?" his speech stammered incoherently, as consternation washed over him. A dawning horror that they thought *he* had done this to his Melissa. "Do you think I did this?" Anxiety and fear rising. "No, I wouldn't do that."

One of the police placed a hand on his shoulder. He shrugged it off, shouting at them, "I didn't do that!! What are you here for?" James lunged to break away from them to get to Melissa. One look from the paramedics stopped him.

"James, we can't do our job if you interfere. Please keep calm. We are taking Melissa to the hospital now. The police are here to assist you."

He watched in anguished silence as the gurney was taken downstairs and Melissa wheeled out of sight.

"Shouldn't I go with her?" he asked, starting to walk to the stairs. "I need to be with her," he turned back, and crumpled, falling onto the floor, sobbing. "I don't understand why you are here," he told the police.

"We are always called in these situations. We are here to help you cope and ensure you are all safe. Why don't I make some coffee?" She spoke quietly but with authority.

"James. Let's go downstairs to the lounge room." said the other one, a man, who gently, but firmly, led James downstairs. "Where are the children, James?"

"I don't know. I came home, and the place was dark. I don't know where the kids are."

"Why don't we look at Melissa's phone to see the last numbers she dialled, and I'm sure we'll find them that way. Thank you," he replied, taking the coffee the policewoman had brought into the room, and then turning his attention back to James, "Tell me where I can find her phone."

"Um, it's usually on the counter in the kitchen, or in her handbag. I'm sorry; I don't know what to do. What will I tell the kids?" James control was fading again, his agitation becoming more pronounced.

The policewoman put her hand on his shoulder. "We will help you with that. We just need you to keep calm, and we'll work it out. Try not to worry about Melissa. She's in the best hands now, and we'll get you to the hospital as soon as possible."

He sat and listened as the ambulance screamed its alarm, creating jagged, ragged holes in the silence; sirens wailing to the night sky, and he wondered if there would be a future with Mel in it.

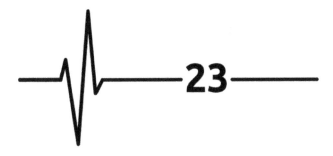

23

James sat on a hard, plastic chair in Melissa's ICU room, idly stroking her hand with his thumb. A distant ambulance shrilled its urgency, as James battled a rush of nausea pushing its way up. All too-fresh memories, bringing a resurgence of fear on a wave of guilt. Shame covered his mind as he realised how far Melissa had fallen. That he had only been focused on himself, and how it all affected him.

"I didn't realise, Honey. I'm so sorry. I just didn't know how terrible it was for you." James' voice strangled as he tried to control himself. "If only I had known. Please, Mel. Please don't give up. Please come back to me. I need you so much. The kids need you." Deep, wracking sobs. "I need you, Mel!" he said again.

There was no other sound in the room except for the unnaturally forced hiss of the intubation machinery; the quiet drip, drip, drip of the IV line into her veins: life-giving air, life-giving fluids. Artificial sustenance.

Hoping, hoping that she would pull through.

He looked up as the Doctor came into the room.

"We have given her the antidote, a receptor antagonist called Flumazenil. She did not respond after the first dosage, so we had to administer a second dose." The doctor delivered the news quietly, but deliberately, preparing James for the possible poor outcome. "If she survives, we will not know for some time whether there will be any brain or organ damage. When we know she is stable, we will put her into an induced coma, which will allow her brain to heal as best it can. With an overdose of this magnitude, the patient can have seizures, as the drugs they've taken leave the body. The induced coma also helps to minimise that possibility. I'm sorry, but we cannot guarantee the outcome. It will be twenty-four hours before we know." He hesitated and then said, "You were lucky to call for help when you did."

James only heard the swish of the curtains, as the doctor left the room. Now, all he could do, all that was left to him, was hope.

Sitting quietly, brushing the tears off his face, listening to the hiss of the ventilator that was keeping Melissa breathing and alive. Watching the ICU nurse doing his checks. Oxygen saturation levels from the probe on her finger. Blood pressure, heart rate, respiratory rate, squiggly lines, and beeping things. James looked at them as though his watching would keep her alive. Bring her back. Yearning, reaching out with his heart; maybe she would be able to feel his love and fight her way back to him.

Floating in a warm light. Silence. Peace.

She stayed quite still, not moving, unsure, just absorbing.

He was sitting over to one side. She could see him. A real presence. Palpable.

Feeling around her, the space felt insubstantial, almost ethereal. And yet, it was at the same time, very solid, just like the man who sat over there, on the branch of the tree.

"Am I dead?" she asked the man. "Is this what it is like to be dead?"

He smiled at her. "Do you want to be dead?"

"Yes. I want to be dead. I can't go back to that." Suddenly, she stopped. "Who are you? Where am I?

What is this place?" Melissa stood up, looking around. "Do I know you? You seem familiar."

"Where do you want to be?" the man asked. He was still sitting on the tree, swinging his legs. Somehow, he looked… and Melissa searched for the word – yes, that was it... he looked free. That was what she wanted. To be free.

And that was what she blurted out, "I want to be free," which startled her. It wasn't something she had consciously understood. She hadn't wanted to die. She just wanted freedom.

The man got off the tree and walked over to her. Every step closer contained a step of dread, and yet at the same time, each step felt closer to hope.

"Melissa," he said. An ocean of love and kindness emanating from him and flowing over her.

Startled, she looked at him. "How do you know who I am?"

"I know all about you. I know all about Grandpop and Ken. I knew you before you were born."

"What? Wait! Are you God or something? Oh, Melissa, get a grip. You don't believe in God." she talked, half to herself, not sure whether she was speaking aloud or catering to random thoughts scattering through her head. "No! God wouldn't let a child go through that crap. I'm hallucinating. I'm not dead. Oh, God! I just want to die."

The man chuckled. "You said a moment ago that you didn't want to die, you just wanted to be free, and now you say you do want to die." Sitting beside her, his face lit up in a smile of amusement. But, it wasn't that he was laughing at her. Somehow, there was complete acceptance of her confusion.

He patted the space beside him. "Why don't you sit down? Do you want to tell me about it?"

"Tell you? You just said you already know! What's to tell?" she sobbed, "All I wanted was, well, I just want it to stop." A strangled half-cry, spoken in utter despair. Pacing, stumbling, grief-laden legs.

He reached for her hand and pulled her down beside himself.

Looking at her, full on, straight in the eyes, his heart's emotions beating in time at her every cry, every feeling showing on his face.

"Who are you anyway? What is this place? If I'm not hallucinating, then what is this? What's happening?" Melissa looked around, seeking answers but seeing nothing except the man beside her. Nothing here except his warmth, the tree he had sat on, and the space around them.

"Do you really want answers, Melissa?" He waited, watching her face, seeing the convulsions of emotion.

They both sat in silence. Melissa struggled to understand.

"I'm hallucinating," she said to herself again, "That's what it is. I didn't take enough pills. It didn't work, and I'm hallucinating. James! Oh, God! Oh, what have I done?! What am I going to do?"

"Why does it matter to you how James is? You left him." the man asked her.

"WHAT! Of course, I care how James is! He's my husband! He supports me when I can't cope." Startled at what she had just revealed to herself, Melissa stopped.

"Oh NO! I didn't want to die, I just wanted to be free! What have I done?! James! Oh, James, what have I done!!" She turned to the man sitting next to her. "Who are you? Am I dreaming? Am I dead? You must be God. Oh, wait… It's part of the hallucination."

"Touch me, Melissa, and see if I'm just a vapour. Have a close look at me." He extended his arms out to her, inviting her to see for herself.

"Sure, I'll enter into this. After all, if you are just my imagination, then it's only a dream and… Ewww, what happened to your hands?! Those are gross scars!"

Melissa recoiled in disgust at the puckered, discoloured flesh that had never healed back into smoothness. She tentatively reached out to touch him, touch the scars, feeling the bumpy, silvery skin indented into his palms.

"You're real!" She stared at him. Disbelief struggling with incredulity. "What is this place! If I'm not hallucinating, what is happening? Who ARE you?"

"I am the Time Weaver, Melissa."

Consternation flickered across her face. "What do you mean by that? What sort of name is Time Weaver?"

"Melissa, I Am, Who was, and is, and is to come."

"Ok," she said. I really am hallucinating. Maybe the whiskey and pills didn't work, and I'm taking the weirdest trip.

The Time Weaver laughed. An infectious, joyous, belly laugh. "Ah, Melissa. I love that about you. I created you with the most amazing joy in your heart, and I am here to see that restored; all that has been stolen, to be given back to you."

She gaped at him; mouth open.

He stared back at her; eyebrows raised in a question. "Well?"

"Somehow, I trust you, Time Weaver, or whoever you are. OK, I'm going to believe what you say, for now anyway. After all, I've got nothing left to lose, I've already lost everything. So, do your damndest then! If you are so great, then show me what James is doing. If you can, that is." She shook her head at herself. *What am I doing? This is just a bad weird dream.* The sense of herself shattered, little pieces frantically spinning around as she tried to make sense of the insensible.

"Melissa, look at me, Beloved. Look at me."

Two pools of misery turned to look at the Time Weaver.

"Beloved," he reached out and stroked her cheek, such a comforting gesture that evoked an eternity of love.

In automatic response, she held that hand to her face, both her hands keeping his there; comfort, understanding and peace flowing into her torment.

"So, you say you didn't want to die; you just wanted 'it' to stop. But, try as you might, you have never been able to stop 'it'. I have seen your counselling. I have heard your anger and rage. I've seen your fights with

James. But nothing has worked, has it? Why don't we try it my way?"

"Your way. What do you mean your way?"

"There is a better way, Melissa. Shall we begin?" He asked her, and she nodded.

Time Weaver waved his hand, wiping aside the block wall of time. She saw herself as though on a giant-screen TV.

THAT time with Grandpop!

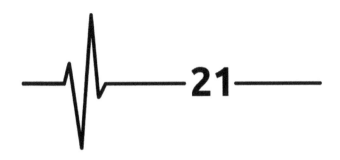

21

School Holidays and a beautiful spring morning. Melissa and Eddie's mother was inside the house, visiting with her parents.

They loved visiting Grams and Grandpop. Their yard backed onto a big lumber supply yard, where Grandpop used to work before he retired. It was always busy: trucks, people, fork hoists. Busy, busy, busy.

But the best part of all was the garage. It was a pirate's treasure chest for children to explore. Melissa loved to stomp on the old organ pedals and listen to the keys wheeze out some notes. When Eddie wound up the old gramophone and put the aged record on it, they would make believe they were old people, listening to the music coming out of the trumpet, and Melissa would bash at the organ, pretending she was a glorious musician.

Today, however, they were outside watching the people at the lumber yard, when Grandpop called.

"Melissa, do you want to come to the store with me?"

Melissa didn't hesitate. To a child of six, it was one of life's big treats, going out with Grandpop to the store. The daily excursion with him to buy the milk, bread and paper, meant you could also be in for some sweets.

She ran inside and grabbed Grandpop's hand, dragging him to the door before he could change his mind.

"Behave yourself," Mummy said. Mummy always said that.

Down the steps – counting them, five steps, down the front path and onto the sidewalk. Holding Grandpop's hand, chattering away, and asking questions. Questions. Melissa was full of questions, always wanting answers to everything.

Grandpop stopped, checked for cars and then they crossed to the other side of the road. This was such an exciting adventure. They even had to cross a railway line, and that was a bit menacing because those trains could drag you under if you weren't careful. Mummy had told her that, so Melissa clung tighter to Grandpop's hand. He would protect her.

After walking for a while, Grandpop said: "Melissa, put your hand in my pocket, there's five cents for you." Five cents was a big deal! It was usually only a few cents. Think of how many sweets five cents could buy! She started to think about aniseed balls and gum-balls and liquorice straps. Sherbet in a packet with a liquorice straw.

"Yes. I told Eddie I would get some sweets if I came with you, Grandpop." skipping alongside, she excitedly put her hand into his pocket, searching for the five-cent coin. There was

nothing in the pocket. In fact, there wasn't even a pocket, it had a big hole in it and all Melissa could find was Grandpop's boy-thing. She baulked at that and yanked her hand out in a hurry. This didn't feel right.

"Grandpop, there's no money in your pocket! You've got a hole in your pocket!" Melissa didn't know what to say or do about her grandfather's penis. Mummy had told her that grownups were to be treated with respect and she must do as they say.

Melissa didn't want to hold Grandpop's hand anymore. She didn't want to be there. She wanted to be at home, where it was safe. She felt a little frozen inside. But there was no choice. They reached the store where they bought the bread, milk, and paper, and Grandpop let her choose her sweets, which she clutched in her small fist all the way home. She had to hold Grandpop's hand. She had to do as she was told. Back past the bus stop. Across the railway line, which suddenly looked even more threatening. Across the road, through the cars and into the house.

She ran through the house, looking for Eddie. Her big brother would be able to explain it. Eddie knew everything. She felt very unsettled. Maybe Grandpop forgot to put his undies on this morning?

Eddie was in the garage. He looked up, as Melissa ran in. "Did you get any sweets, Liss?" he asked. He stopped at the look on Melissa's face. "What? Did you do something naughty? Is Mummy going to be angry with you?"

Melissa's long, chestnut-brown ponytail was coming out, and she tossed her hair aside, impatiently. "Eddie, Grandpop was really strange this morning. He told me there was five cents in his pocket, but when I put my hand in to get it, there was nothing there but a hole and his boy-thing. It felt strange, Eddie. I didn't know what to do. I don't like it."

Turning back to the project he was exploring, Edward's face looked troubled. "I don't know, Liss. I don't do that stuff. Do you think Mummy will be angry?"

As she wandered out to the back yard by herself, Melissa was thinking hard. If Eddie didn't say anything, and she didn't say anything, maybe Grandpop wouldn't say anything either, and then she wouldn't get into trouble. Mummy always told her that no one was allowed to play with her bottom. She guessed that meant she wasn't allowed to play with anyone else's bottom either.

She sat outside playing daisy chains and just looking at things in the garden. Her sweets were forgotten in her confusion.

Then Mummy called, "Edward! Melissa! It's time we went home. Melissa, you left your sweets on the table."

As Melissa went inside to say goodbye to her grandparents and get her bag of sweets, she was glad that Grandpop was with Grams in the kitchen. She got her sweets and started out the door to the car. "Melissa, aren't you going to say goodbye to Grams and Grandpop?" Mummy asked her. Melissa waved *her hand at her grandparents. "Bye, see you next time!" and ran out to get in the car.*

Her mother just shrugged at her parents, "Kids," she said.

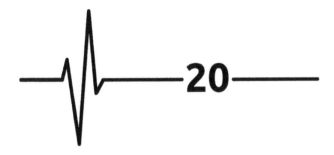

—20—

"Oh! I had forgotten about that." Melissa stared as the scene faded away. She put her head between her knees, nausea rising; battling the dizzy, drifting sensation in her head.

Time Weaver made no move to touch her. He stood beside her, a strong, reassuring presence, waiting until she was ready to continue. "What happened then, Melissa? What happened to that little you?"

"He shouldn't have done that! How dare he do that!" She was angry. "I trusted him; he was my grandfather!"

"Yes, he was your grandfather, and you should have been able to trust him. Unfortunately, the world of man is so corrupt that little children are often not safe, and it is not right, is it? What should I do with

51

him?" Time Weaver asked her a question, forcing her to dig a little deeper.

"Do with him? He's dead. What can you do with him! I'm GLAD he's dead."

"Melissa, if I'm the Time Weaver, shouldn't I be able to do what I want?"

"Not even Superman can bring back the dead! I hope he rots." She spoke in disgust. "My own grandfather! What was wrong with him! You don't do that to kids!"

Time Weaver nodded. "No. He should not have done that," and then with a huge grin and a raised eyebrow, he said, "Superman?"

"He should have loved me and protected me." Angry words spilling out. She yelled at Time Weaver, "You men. You are all the same. Destroy little children, use them as playthings!" Fists clenched, mouth clenched, her whole body rigid in an effort to control the surging emotions.

Putting his hand under her chin, Time Weaver tilted her head up, so that she was looking directly at him. "Look at me, Little One.

Deep brown eyes, fathomless depths, eyes which saw and knew, and loved.

"Do you see how instinctively you knew that what Grandpop did was wrong? Every person is born with a conscience, which they can choose to either listen to or ignore, hardening their hearts and falling gradually into greater depravity. You have done it yourself, Melissa. All of mankind has the ability to listen to me."

She was quiet, thinking about what Time Weaver had said. "Yes, you are right. We make choices, don't we? And those choices lead us." She sat with bent knees, head on hands, staring away into a distant memory.

"Yes," she said, "I can see what you are saying. Sometimes, I would go to do something, and a little voice inside me would caution me not to, but I'd do it anyway because I was either angry or drunk or feeling rebellious."

"How did that work out for you then, Mel?" Time Weaver was doing his gentle digging again.

She laughed. "Lousy. I just made things worse. I guess if I had listened to that little voice telling me not to do something, then life would be a whole lot easier."

He just nodded and said, "Oh, yes. It definitely would. Do you remember me telling you not to drink that whiskey, and not to take those pills?"

She looked at him, stunned. "You knew?" and solemnly, nodding, continued, "But I didn't listen, did I?"

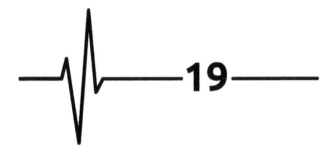

19

James fumbled in his pocket for his cell phone. There really wasn't any news to tell her parents. They would be beyond anxious. There were three messages from them, which he ignored; instead, dialling his mother-in-law's phone.

"James? Is there any news?" His mother-in-law had been crying, her voice sounding as though stuffed up with a cold.

"Hi, Ma, I'm still at the hospital. Mel is still unconscious, but they say she is stabilising." He listened to the voice at the other end, trying to think how to calm her parents.

"Amy told me to tell you she is praying, and she has her entire church praying. Even though I think her religiousness is over the top, right now, I will take any help we can get." She paused just long enough to change timbre into a whine, "Why does Melissa have to be so dramatic? In my day, we didn't talk about things like this. She just needs to let it go!"

James gritted his teeth. "Thanks, Ma. If I hold the phone to Mel's ear, would you like to say something? You know how they say that people in a coma can hear what people are saying?" James was grasping at anything he could think of. He didn't want to talk to anyone, didn't want to hear that Melissa's religious sister had got the whole world involved in their private affairs. Didn't want to hear Ma-in-law trotting out the same old 'let it go' stuff.

"No. Not at the moment, James. I don't think I would be able to cope with that. Not talking to my dead daughter when she can't respond."

"She's NOT dead!! And stop saying that! She's just in a coma." He hated Ma-in-law's negativity. "Ahh, I need to go and phone my parents now. I'll call as soon as there's any information." Grateful to stop the conversation, he pressed the end button, before she could carry on.

His hands were shaking. Anxiously checking Mel's monitors. Trying to understand what it all meant. Dialling his parents, hoping that just the sound of their voices would bring peace. "Dad, hi. There's no change yet. The doctor said he will put her into an induced coma when she is stable."

"I love you, Son. Melissa is strong, and we know she's had mental problems recently. It wasn't fair what she went through as a child. But we'll get through this together. Have you spoken to the kids?" His Dad was so calming, reassuring, but even he didn't understand the gaping wound in Mel. That generation refused to look at it. But at least he wasn't dramatic, like Ma-in-law.

"No, I haven't spoken to them. I told the neighbour what had happened and she's happy to keep them there. If she gets worse, then we'll bring the kids in to say goodbye." James lost his brittle self-control, his voice just a whisper, as he swallowed convulsively, struggling to speak. "I'm going now, Dad. Love you."

The disconnect click sounded loud in the ensuing silence.

"Would you like to get yourself a cup of tea or coffee?" The ICU nurse looked at him, seeing his effort at normality and knowing from experience how to deal with it. "There are facilities just down the hall. Come on, I'll show you where it is."

"NO! That means you have to leave Mel!" James fear lurched out of him before he could rationalise it.

"She's ok for a few minutes. If anything happens in that time, I will hear it. The monitors she's hooked up to will give plenty of loud warning."

"If you're sure she'll be ok? I am hungry. I didn't get any dinner."

"She'll be ok. I won't leave her while you are gone." The ICU nurse gently persuaded James to leave. "The Doctor is due in at about 10 pm to reassess Melissa, so be back before then."

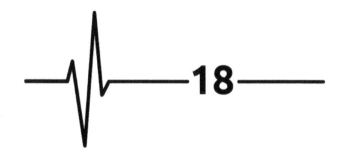

Time Weaver looked at Melissa.

"Mankind thinks they can control everything around them. They think they can do without Creator. How did that go for you, Melissa?"

She looked at him blankly. "What do you mean?"

"In the beginning" he started, "Man was the most precious of all creation. Until he decided that he didn't need us."

"What?" a moment where perplexity gave way to truth, sinking deep, joining with embedded truth. "Wait! You are saying you are God? Seriously? No!" she said, shaking her head. "No, I don't believe in God. Arrrghh! What is going on?!"

"No, you don't believe in God, and yet every time you are amazed, or in fear, or angry or any other emotion, the first thing that comes out of your mouth, is 'Oh my God'. Maybe there is a vestige of something deep inside that is continually revealing the truth to you. But again, you are not listening." He looked at her questioningly. "You said that Melissa, not me. You said to me, 'I didn't listen, did I?' So, are you going to listen to me now?"

She looked momentarily confused, then embarrassed. "I'm sorry, I've been swearing and talking about stuff that church people don't like. Sorry. Me and my potty-mouth."

Time Weaver started laughing. "Oh, Melissa, that is such a perverted religious way of thinking. How sad, that in front of those who love you the most, that you feel you have to be on your very best behaviour. Don't you know that my love for you transcends all that junk?" He went very quiet. "My sweet Melissa. Let's talk about the reason you are here. You have tried to live your life without me. You have tried everything to get rid of the pain inside you. What caused that pain? In the same way that a surgeon has to cut and cause pain in order to heal, we also need to look at and examine what happened in your life. Then, we can apply MY healing to it."

She considered for a while and, in a very tiny voice, said, "I don't want to think about it. I didn't think about it for years, and then decided to 'do the right thing and think about it,' and look where that got me."

He smiled at her, that delightful smile that encompassed her in her entirety, bringing complete acceptance. "My sweet girl, you tried to do everything you could, but you did it without me. Did you know that you are here now because other people have been talking to me about you?"

"Really!" she was startled. "Who?"

"Well, shall we start with Amy? I showed Amy who I really am. She delights me so much with her enthusiasm and passion for me. Even now, Melissa, in her love for you, she is calling everyone she can think of, to pray for you."

"But those people she hangs out with, are nuts! They don't do church properly! Whoever heard of going to church and having fun!" She spluttered. "Do you know that they dance and, and, they shout. Shouldn't church be quiet and, and, well, you know." she finished lamely. "If you don't do everything right, God would be so mad. It's not worth even starting."

The Time Weaver gave a great shout of laughter. "Do you really think that in order to please God, that you have to behave in a certain way, and do church in the right manner?" He then looked very serious. "Religion is a cruel taskmaster! Did you know that in the Holy Writings which mankind calls the 'Old Testament,' there are two thirds more feasts than days of fasting and mourning? Does that sound like a rigid and boring life or an angry God?" He put his head to one side and looked at her, smiling, eyes crinkled in laughter. "I know you like to party, Melissa. I have walked through some of your parties with your friends and seen and heard what was being said and done. Did it help you? Did getting drunk or smoking your weed and the other drugs make the pain go away?" In an ocean of understanding, the Time Weaver laid bare her life.

She was very, very still. The unveiling of her heart caught in that fraction of a breath.

"Melissa, shall we look at what caused your heart to be so broken?"

"If you want," she said, very hesitantly. "But you won't like it. You shouldn't see that." The agony in her heart, showing in her words. "Do we have to?" She blurted out. "I have already looked at it so often. With my friends, my counsellor. It just doesn't do any good."

"No, it doesn't, because you are looking at it through the lens of pain and time, not the complete overview of what lies beyond."

Tortured pain suddenly passed through the Time Weaver. Slow tears rolled down his face. "I was there," he whispered to her. "I saw it all; what was done to you, was done to me. Stay close to me always, Melissa. I bear your burdens."

She didn't notice he was holding her hand, tightly.

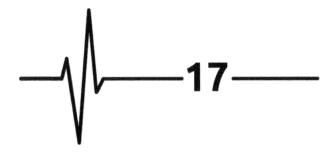

Melissa was so happy to share her birthday with her big cousin Ken. Even though he was a lot older than her, she felt special, almost grown up, because she was included in his birthday celebration. The adults thought it was cute the way 18-year-old Ken wanted to see his little cousin and share a birthday dinner, with their birthdays just one day but ten years apart.

There was nothing unusual about Ken coming to see Aunt and Uncle and taking Melissa for ice cream. Nothing suspicious to the adults.

Time Weaver moved closer to Melissa. "You trusted him," he said. "And he abused that trust."

"Yes," she answered.

Ken arrived unannounced one day, proud to show Melissa's Daddy his new car, red with a white stripe down the side. Daddy and Ken opened the hood and poked at the engine, talked stuff

Melissa didn't understand. Their hands were dirty with grease. Mummy made them wash their hands before coming inside.

"Melissa, do you want to go for a ride in my new car?" Ken asked his little cousin.

"Mummy, may I go with Ken?"

"Sure honey. Don't be too long will you Ken" Mummy told him.

She felt so special, sitting up front, waving at her friends as Ken drove to the park. She loved the park, where she and Eddie would play for hours; their friends joining them for games. Hide 'n' seek in the bushes, many bushes, secluded places, where children could go and sit and think, or play with their friends.

Ken asked Melissa to show him her special hiding place, the place where she was alone and could not be seen by the other kids. Happily, she skipped along, showing him the quiet enclosure, almost inside a clump of bushes. Not overlooked by houses, a real spot of seclusion.

"Is this it then, Melissa?" he asked.

"Yes, no one bothers me here. I can play and read and sit and think."

Ken scanned the area, noting the absence of being able to be seen. "It really is a place to be alone and private, isn't it?" he said.

Melissa sat down in her special place. Happy. Alone with her cousin. Happy to show him her own place.

"You know I love you, don't you, Melissa?"

"Yes, and I love you too, Ken."

"Only girls I really love, get to do this with me, Melissa."

"Oh, I know. And Ken, I really love you!" She grabbed his arm and hugged it tightly.

"It's only really special girls that I really love, who I show this to, Melissa," Ken said, as he was stroking her hair, "Girls who I can trust. Can you keep a secret?"

"Yes, I can keep a secret for you, Ken." Melissa looked up at her cousin, adoration in her eyes.

Slowly, Ken unzipped his fly. Melissa watched puzzled. He brought his boy-thing out. Melissa's brothers had boy-things too, but they didn't look like this.

"Touch it, Mel."

Shocked, and with an automatic reaction, her hands flew behind her back, fingers tightly woven together. "No! Ken. Mummy said I'm not allowed to touch anyone else's bottom!"

"It's ok, Mel. It's our secret. Remember, you said you would keep my secret." Taking hold of her arm, untangling her tense hands, he pulled her closer to him. "Touch it, lick it, you will

like it. You know how I love you. You love me, too, don't you?"
Ken grabbed Melissa's head and shoved his erect penis into her
mouth.

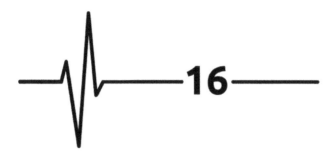

16

Time Weaver stood close to Melissa. She was rigid, shaking in reaction.

"He took your innocence and childhood away, didn't he?" It wasn't so much a question as a statement. "He stole your days to come."

All she could do was nod.

"He lied and cheated and pulled you on a rubber band, telling you he loved you, and then abused that love and trust. He had power over you. Now, someone inadvertently twangs on that rubber band, and you feel compelled to respond. You feel guilty and then push the other person to confirm that their love is genuine and that you are OK.

"That, in turn, ensured that even today, you do not trust anyone, even me. For you are sure there is an ulterior motive to someone's kindness; that they want something of you. All your life, you have sought to control everything around you so you could feel safe. Fear goes hand in hand with guilt. And loneliness presides over all. Although you love James and believe he loves you, that love is tainted with unforgiveness and lack of trust. In a strange way, you hold James responsible for your pain."

Sobbing, Melissa buried her face in her hands. Every word Time Weaver had spoken, was as a shard of light straight into her heart, illuminating the hidden things.

He turned her to himself and gathered her in his arms, holding her safe. Close to his heart, so she could hear the rhythm of the beat, comforting, and secure.

"How can I break free of this, then?" her voice muffled from being buried in his chest.

Holding her at arm's length away from him so she could see him, his eyes searched her face. "The crux of healing lies in forgiveness."

Melissa stumbled back, away from him, then ran back, screaming, "Forgiveness! Give me a good reason why I should forgive him! How dare you say that? How dare you ask me to forgive that...that....pig! I hate him! How can you even suggest that! I hate him. Do you understand? He took everything of me. He took my self. He took me."

Her sobs filled the emptiness and echoed through his heart. All the anguish for the past decades lived under this tempest, tore out of her. "This is why I want to die. I can't bear this anymore. It's not fair, it's just not fair." A little girl lost and alone in a storm, not understanding, not understood.

"You have tried so hard to be brave. You have tried to be stoical and reason it all out. But it doesn't work, does it?"

"No," she sniffed, "I have tried hard. I watch other people and copy what they do because surely, they know the correct way to act. Maybe I can be accepted that way. But I'm not accepted. It doesn't matter what I do, it's always wrong. I can't win, and so here I am, with you."

He took her by the hand and led her back to the tree, and as though she was just a little girl again, lifted her up so that she was sitting on the branch. He swung himself up next to her and put his arm around her shoulders. She nestled into the reassuring comfort.

"You know that rubber band that keeps twanging you back?" he asked.

"Mmmm, yes. Every time I think I've conquered something, there it goes again."

"The only way to cut that rubber band forever is to forgive."

She started to protest, but he held his hand up. "Let me finish, and then you can tell me off. Is that a deal?"

Glaring at him angrily, Melissa nodded.

"Being attached to that rubber band is a bit liked a barbed wire fence. Let's say you are on a farm. There are so many animals, and you are keen to look more closely at them, so you lean over the fence, taking hold of it as you do so. Almost immediately, you notice pain in your hands and look down to see that you have clutched hold of a barbed wire fence. It hurts! It hurts a lot, and it is cutting your hands. What would the sensible thing be to do?"

"Well, let go, of course. Duh!" she spat at him.

"Yes. The sensible thing would be to let go. But, let's just suppose you keep holding onto the barbed wire. It keeps cutting you painfully, and you cry because of the pain. When you do finally let the barbed wire go, while the cuts are still there, they eventually heal, and yes, there are scars, but the pain is gone."

"Yes, and so, what has that to do with me? Rubber bands? Forgiveness?" A torrent of anger poured out of Melissa. She jumped off the branch and paced around. "What has that to do with anything, other than the person hanging onto the fence is an idiot!"

Stroking his beard, Time Weaver sat and watched her for a while. He never interrupted her, quietly waiting until she had finished.

"WELL?" she yelled at him.

"Well?" he repeated back at her. "Well actually, it has everything to do with unforgiveness and rubber bands and you. You see, unforgiveness leaves you attached to the pain and anger. It's the rubber band that keeps twanging you back, repeatedly." He held his hand up again. "Hear me out. Melissa. Then tell me if I'm wrong. What unforgiveness does, is to constantly remind you of what happened. It gives you an excuse to walk around, feeling continually angry. Over time, it not only damages your health, but it destroys you. Forgiveness, Beloved, is not for the other person. Forgiveness is to set *you* free."

Quizzically, her head tilted on one side, she looked at him.

"Practicing forgiveness starts in your mind. Sometimes, in as little time as a minute, you may have to forgive ten times, but the better you get at practising it, the further apart the minutes get. In forgiving, you are breaking the power the other person has over you. It ceases to control you. You are choosing to remove the power of the act over your emotions. You are saying, 'I no longer hold you accountable for my emotions.' As long as you are holding a person accountable for your pain, you are empowering that hurt, that action to have authority in your life. It continues to bind you. By the act of forgiveness, you are breaking that bond and releasing me and giving me authority to come in, and start the process of healing."

Pain so evident, showing in every nuance, every plane of her face, in the way she held herself. "Yes, I can see that. Yes, I can." She closed her eyes as her face crumpled. Wailing in despair, "But why? Why does he get off completely, and I am left for the rest of my life to carry this? Why? Isn't there any justice for me? He goes on and lives his life in his comfortable home with his comfortable wife and children. But for me? My husband has to listen to my agony. He puts up with my dysfunction, and my children have only a partially capable mother! Where is the justice in that?"

"We, my Father and I, have seen the pain this has caused, and I want you to know, that we know. Watch with me a little." He waved at the screen again.

Ken and Melissa were at her favourite hiding place, down in the big park. As she watched, she saw herself, standing just an arms span away, facing Ken. He was manipulating her again. But something was different about this picture. In between the two of them, just off to Melissa's left, stood Time Weaver. He was closer to Melissa than to Ken, and he was looking at Ken with such great sadness, that it made Melissa want to weep.

"Forgiveness is not for him, it is for you, to free you from this entanglement. There is a saying in the sacred annals of Heaven - if anyone causes one of these little ones to stumble, it would be better for them to have a large millstone hung around their neck and to be drowned in the depths of the sea. We care so very much about you and what happened."

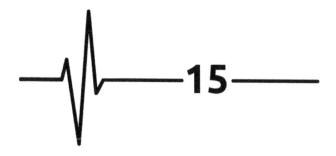

15

Having eaten an unsatisfying burger, James hurried back to Melissa's room, along the quiet hospital corridors, fearful, in case anything should happen while he was gone; afraid that he would miss the Doctor.

Everything in him was crying out to FIX IT, but he was as helpless in this web as she was. At least her breathing, even if it were artificial, was normal, unlike when he had found her. At least her skin was pink again and not that horrible pale colour.

James startled out of his thoughts, as the Doctor came in. He watched him as he read Melissa's notes the nurse had been taking. The Doctor walked over to Melissa, opened an eyelid and shone his torch directly into the eye, watching for any change, any hope that healing was happening.

Taking a deep breath, or was it a sigh, the Doctor sat next to James. "She is stable now. We would expect her to start to come out of the coma soon. However, we have no way of knowing how much brain damage has been done. Before I put her into an induced coma, I would like to ascertain the brain function. To do that, we need to do a C.A.T. scan. I will schedule that and pending the outcome," the Doctors voice drifted off, leaving a myriad of unspoken words. "Well," the doctor shrugged, "then I will make a decision."

"If she's coming out of the overdose coma, why do you need to put her back into a coma? Won't that make it worse?" James was perplexed, clearly just wanting Mel to wake up, everything to go back to being normal.

"Because it is the best way to allow the brain to heal. When someone is put into an induced coma, it is the same as when they are under a general anaesthetic. We use a drug called Propofol. It allows the brain to rest and provides the patient with time to heal. Our biggest concern right now is what brain function she has. As I said, we will have to do a C.A.T. scan to find that out. He stood up tiredly. "Maybe you should go home and get some rest. We will be putting her into the coma for at least 12 to 15 hours. As with all medical procedures, it is not without risk. The main things we have to watch for is that her blood pressure doesn't fall too low and that her circulation is maintained. However, because the coma will be a relatively short one, I do not foresee any complications."

"What if her brain is damaged?" James struggled to get the words out but felt he just had to know. Was Mel still there? A coldness settled on him.

"We won't know until after the C.A.T. scan results. That will tell us, that if she survives, whether she will come out of the coma in a vegetative state or not. We will be continuing to monitor her brain waves." Pointing to the screen, he showed James the section showing the lines that looked like the seismograph of an earthquake. He hesitated. "Do you know if Melissa was a donor? Please think about donating her organs, if the C.A.T. scan comes back negative." An awkward pause finishing on, "I'm so sorry." And the doctor left the room.

When will I ever feel normal again? When will this feeling of rocks ever get out of my gut? James thought. "God," he prayed, silently, "God, we don't really talk. I don't even know if you are there, and if you are there, whether you would listen to me. But please. I'm begging you. Please bring Mel back to me. I will go to church, I will even put money in the plate, just bring her back."

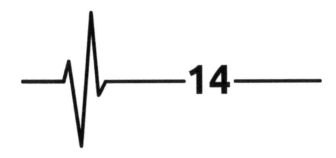

There it was. A child again. Unable to speak up.
Unable to move. A prisoner of her past. Frozen in
time.

The yawning chasm of past manipulation lying at
her feet. Just one step. One step to slide down into the
blackness.

"Oh my God, Oh my God, Oh my God!" She
gasped, panting, hyperventilating in panic.

She clung onto Time Weaver, fear's tendrils seeking
to freshly ensnare her heart, gripping mind and
emotions. Tangled filth threatening to engulf and
overthrow her tenuous control.

"From that point on, he manipulated and
controlled you, didn't he?" Time Weaver's voice
slowly penetrated her consciousness. "It was easy to

make you believe you were the one at fault, that you were a naughty, dirty little girl."

Desperately clinging to Time Weaver, shaking outside as her insides shivered, quaked, trembled like convulsions of jelly threatening to disintegrate.

"For four years, he systematically stripped you of your dignity and self-worth, destroying the essence of your freedom. It ripped at your emotional foundations and twisted your ability to see yourself in truth." His voice was very quiet, full of a world of compassion.

Choking on her emotions, Melissa sank to the ground and curled into a ball, no longer able to hold on. No escaping, screaming inside her head. Concrete statue face.

"It destroyed your foundations, so that the knowledge of who you are, has been distorted. All that you should have been was shattered, and you have lived with that brokenness all these years." He knelt beside her, one hand resting lightly on her back. "I have come to give you life, and to give it to you abundantly. First, though, we need to rebuild your foundations, make them strong and secure."

Panting, shallow breathing, Melissa clenched her fists tighter. "Can you do that?" she gasped in a very small voice, barely audible, afraid even to consider that future.

"The question is not whether I can, it's will you trust me?" He answered.

"But *how* can you do that?" Melissa sat up, tears and snot intermingling. "It happened so many years ago." Giving a great gulp of a sob, she said, "It seems I'm consigned to the junk heap for the rest of my life."

He reached out to her and turned her face to his. "I'm the *Time Weaver*. What do those two words mean? Melissa, I was, before you were. I am now, and I will be long after your body has returned to the earth. I am the TIME Weaver."

She considered that for a while. A puzzled look flitted across her face, "You mean, you can like um, bend time? Like Dr. Who, travelling through time?"

"Oh! You are so funny! Yes, I suppose if you want to use that analogy. But let's put it this way, I am OUTSIDE of time. I created it."

She sat still, considering.

"I can't undo what has been done. Mankind, in their free will, chose that path, but the damage done to you, I can, and really want to heal. The question again is, will you trust me?"

Trust. She thought. I don't trust anyone. I don't even really trust James.

"No." He said. You can't trust anyone." He smiled at her astonishment at his understanding of her thoughts. "Trust is the main issue. So I ask you again. Will you be willing to trust me?"

Her heart pounded, fear releasing an adrenaline rush, sweat beading on her forehead, nausea rising. Memories of Kens' twisting of her childish love and trust.

"If I trust you, will you promise not to hurt me again?" she asked, her voice tiny, child-like, the days of her fractured and splintered life all rushing together to one dot of a moment. Terror of exposure threatening to shut down the tiny, fragile, seed of hope.

"Melissa, I am not a man that I would lie to you. I cannot lie. I am the Way, I am Truth, and I hold your life safely in my hands. I am Trust. You can trust me, Little One."

Just as a snail dares to seek out the world around it through coming out of its shell, seeking for predators in its surrounds, carefully, gradually, Melissa forced the fear down, looking at Time Weaver, trying to see any deceit, any ulterior intention.

He stayed still, allowing her time to test his motives.

"OK," she finally said. "OK, but Oh God, I'm so scared." She stayed very still for a while, thinking hard, weighing it up. Inhaling and breathing out slowly, she whispered: "So, how do we correct my foundations then?"

Holding out one of those hideous scarred hands to pull her to her feet, He said, "It is only as you see yourself reflected in me, that your foundations will come into right alignment.

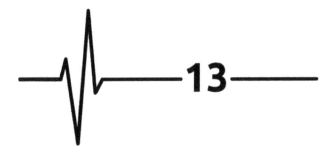

13

It was after one in the morning when James parked the car in the garage for the second time that night. Wearily he got out and opened the door to the house, momentarily blinded by the lights. He had left them on in his panic to get to Melissa. Oscar was frantic, winding and weaving in front of him, his plaintiff meow seeking to gain attention.

"Oh, Oscar, puss. I'm so sorry. I forgot to feed you, before. You will be so hungry, boy." Reaching for the cat food, turning the kettle on, James didn't notice for just a moment, how quiet the house was. When the cat had satisfied his hunger, and the kettle stopped boiling, the intense, lonely silence pressed into his exhaustion. Ignoring the hot water, he slowly climbed the stairs, switching lights off as he went.

Alone in their room, he stood and stared at where Melissa had so recently been. He couldn't bear to be there, but it was more than he could do to leave. Sighing. In slow-motion. With aching emotional debilitation, he shuffled to the bathroom and turned the shower on. Leaving his clothes where they fell, he just stood under the water, as it flowed over him, mingling with his tears.

Suddenly, he remembered his cell phone was downstairs in the kitchen where he had dumped the keys as he came in. Hurrying, drying off quickly, running down the stairs, hoping to hear the phone ringing to say, *'A miracle, she is awake,'* but the blank screen just stared back at him; 1:30am.

Dreading being in that bed without her, and dreading not being close to where he could smell *her* smell on the pillow; undecided, hesitant about what to do, he finally pulled on pyjamas, pulled the covers back and climbed in, turning the bedside lamp off. That interminably lonely bed. He reached for her pillow and inhaled as though the smell of her would keep her alive.

Guilt crawled into his mind and took over. Could I have stopped her from doing this? Why didn't I see the signs? I've been so selfish. Now, what am I going to do! Oh, Mel, my Love. He started thumping his pillow, which suddenly felt full of stones, judgmental, pointing at his inadequacies. Lying on his back and staring at the darkened ceiling; thoughts chasing each other around. What if she doesn't survive? What if she is a vegetable? What will I tell Ben & Alex? How will we cope? I will have to get after-school care for them. What about money?! It will all take more money! How will I be able to pay for it all, the mortgage, childcare? Chaos in shards of uncertainty.

Endless questioning, unanswered why's, his mind overwhelmed with draining fears, he finally dropped into an exhausted sleep.

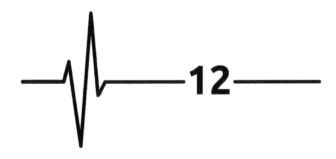

"I don't understand any of this," she said. "I don't know what is happening. You have told me you are the Time Weaver, but I don't know what that means. But I kind of know you. Something inside me says, 'I know you, but I've never met you before.'" She looked at him curiously, trying to figure out how she knew him. Then shaking her head, continued, "I know that my life has been chaos, and it doesn't matter what I do, I can't change. And now you are saying you can change it all." She wailed in despair. "I've done everything else, and nothing has worked, so I guess I have nothing left to lose. I have no idea where I am or what is going on, so I figure I'm out of my own options." She stood facing Time Weaver.

He listened, and it seemed as she spoke, that He absorbed the energy of her brokenness inside Himself.

"Mankind has tried so many different ways to erase their own feelings of ineptitude and brokenness. They have filled the void that I belong in, with so much busy-ness. You have tried the spectrum of them as well." He turned to her abruptly, snapping the curl of fear that was invading her spirit.

As though released from a trance, Melissa blinked, aware again of Time Weaver. With an outward whoosh of breath, releasing a laden sigh, she said, "So, when do we start? How do I see myself reflected in you?"

"I was hoping you would say that, my Beloved. Shall we sit back on that branch and watch a movie together?"

"What! A movie? I thought we were going to sort out this rubble of my life!" Her mouth pursed in perplexity, tinged with anger.

"Yes, a movie. Remember I said, 'It is only as you see yourself reflected in me, that your foundations will come into right alignment?" Waggling his eyebrows comically, he took her hand and led her over to the tree.

Doing that hand waving thing again, the giant TV screen appeared. She watched, as a wavery, watery, chaotic mess appeared in front of them.

"In the beginning," Time Weaver announced, "we created what would be termed heavens and this beautiful planet earth." His voice was full of yearning. "We created it all for you, Melissa, and for all people, whom we created in our image. We made the sky with the sun and the moon, the stars and planets, galaxies and universes and then, little planet earth. All because we wanted to have the companionship of our beloved children - you."

As he talked, that which was being spoken appeared on the screen. She watched in fascination as scene after scene slid across in front of her. The explosion of light as the earth was formed. Stars and planets placed in the night sky, each in their own sphere and each precisely in their own orbits, all interlocking and interacting with the other.

"The earth is incredibly precious to us. It was made in complete perfection so that mankind would never know want or disease. No deprivation of any description. My Father and I walked in the most beautiful garden with the first of mankind. Every day, Father would share their day with them and teach them of His ways, teach them the ways of the galaxies and of His kingdom. There was no terror, no cruelty, nothing at all to fear. The atmosphere was in perfect balance for our beautiful children to live and enjoy. Food was abundant, and the animals we had made roamed freely and content with each other."

Melissa watched, astounded as animals interacted with man-kind, communicating and living together. Lions lay down with lambs. Enormous dinosaurs stepping carefully around the tiniest of creatures. Gentleness and love overlaid the entire earth. "Is this what they call Eden?" she asked him.

"Yes, this was Eden. This was what we created and made for you all to live together in, so that we might enjoy your company and show you how much you are loved." A great sadness washed across his face. "We gave man free will. For what good is it, if we created an entire race that was little more than robots? How could one love and have companionship with something that is merely programmed to react in a certain way?"

"Well, no, you can't. Even my cat Oscar knows and interacts with me. But my dishwasher machine, I guess that's a kind of robot. I can't talk to that. Well I can," she grinned, "When it doesn't do what it's programmed to do, then I talk to it. Well yell at it actually and probably kick it, and then call the repairman."

Time Weaver laughed at the picture she created with her words. "Yes, exactly. So, we gave mankind free will to interact with us. We poured our love out on them. And then they rejected us."

"What! Why would anyone do that? Melissa was startled and taken aback at that concept. Shc felt so comforted and complete with Time Weaver.

"You did, Melissa."

"I did?! But I had never met you before this, all this .... whatever this place is," she said, waving her hands around at the inexplicable surroundings, "before all this happened!" she finished.

"Oh, but you have met us before, Melissa. Watch."

She turned back to the screen, enthralled with this wonderful creation, the beautiful garden, and interaction between mankind and animals. On occasion, Time Weaver would be in the garden with them all, sometimes sitting and watching. And sometimes joining in the fun. The man and woman's DNA was brilliant in its clarity, glowing with the purity of unpolluted life. Every strand reflected in the face of the Time Weaver, his own DNA the patriarch of theirs. The strands of laminin glowing in a beautiful † shape.

"Just watch," he whispered.

The scenes continued across the screen.

A beautiful creature, the likes of which she had never seen before, wafted ethereally through the garden and came up to the woman. Smiling at her as she reached out and stroked it, murmuring loving words, the creature nestled into her.

It spoke to the woman, and Melissa could hear its beautiful voice, melodious, like a myriad of crystal bells singing in the breeze. "Did Creator really say that you are not to eat of that tree in the middle of the garden?" it asked Eve.

The woman smiled at the creature. "Yes, He did. You know that already." She continued to stroke it, enjoying the moment. "We can eat of anything in the garden, but not that tree, for Creator said, if we do, then we shall surely die."

"Shall we go and look at it, Eve?" The creature moved off a little way. The woman followed it. "Do you really think that Creator actually meant that? Don't you think he meant something different? Look how beautiful and desirable the fruit is. I don't think he really meant that. He meant that when the time is right, you can eat of it and then you will be as gods also. I'm sure it will be good to eat."

Melissa watched mesmerized as the woman was manipulated and played by the creature.

The woman reached out and took a fruit from the tree, looking around a little guiltily to ensure Creator wasn't watching. She bit into it. The man came up to her "What are you doing! You know we aren't allowed to eat that."

"Oh no, it is so good and so delicious!" The juice was dripping off her chin. "I am sure Creator only meant that we weren't to eat too much of it." And she handed the fruit to the man, who also ate it.

Melissa cried out, an involuntary cry. "No!" Turning to Time Weaver, she said, "Why didn't you stop it?!"

"How can I, Melissa? I gave you free will. Mankind chose rebellion and disobedience. From that moment on, manipulation and all vile things entered into our perfect, beautiful world. We gave you free will."

"But, I didn't do that! Why do I have to suffer for what they did!" Melissa was indignant.

"Watch Melissa, watch again," he said.

The scene changed as the garden withdrew from the man and the woman. Where there had been no effort, only rest, humanity toiled to live. The ground now grew thorns and was hard to break up. Food wasn't abundant; they had to work hard for it. A sensation previously unknown, pain, entered into their world. The man and woman watched as two of their sons fought, and one killed the other.

As Melissa followed what was happening on the screen, the woman and the man were overlaid with DNA symbols and outlines. The DNA gradually grew corrupted and tainted. Woman after woman, man after man, passing in brief sensory bombardment, DNA and minds degrading. Man subjugating man, denigrating woman, killing one another and spoiling the land. The land cried out in agony at each drop of illegally spilt blood. Animals destroyed and whole species wiped out. Despicable acts; man against man, woman against woman and children being used, abused and murdered. The perfect DNA that had been put in the human race started to grow hazy and distorted. Disease and poverty. Earthquakes, famines, volcanic eruptions. The earth groaned in its destruction, as stars and planets ceased their singing and started to die. Faster and faster, thousands upon millions of people flitting past, all coming from the same initial two, all bearing the same DNA, which grew ever more perverted.

"STOP!" She shrieked at the Time Weaver. "Stop it. Please stop it!" She scrunched her eyes tight shut, and her hands flew to cover her ears.

He held his hand up, and the motion paused, leaving the screen with aeons of women stretching back, flitting DNA frozen on the screen, showing Melissa in the foreground, all her ancestors reaching behind her. Each a part of the other. Melissa, mother, grandmother, great grandmother, each an access of life to the other, her DNA, her culpability in the downfall of mankind.

"I can't stand that! Why did you allow that to happen?" She was sobbing.

"Beloved." Time Weaver looked at her with great understanding. "Beloved." He said again. "We bound ourselves to our own laws, which gave mankind their own choices, and this is the consequence of man choosing death over life. Your own pain is the consequence of what happened way back then. What James is suffering is the consequence of others' choice to abuse you, and then your choice in drinking that whiskey and swallowing all those pills."

She stared at him in horror. "The human race is completely stuffed then, isn't it?" she whispered, "There's absolutely no hope for us. Everything you've shown me, all the disgusting, perverted things," shaking her head, as her voice trailed off. "There's no hope!" Swinging around to Time Weaver, she cried, "My children! What hope do they have?"

"None. There is no hope at all, outside of me. None at all." He said.

Appalled, Melissa stared at him and got off the branch they had been sitting on. She paced around; four metres this way; abruptly changing direction, one metre. Stopping again, five paces; stopping, staring into nothing.

Time Weaver sat and watched her.

She suddenly stopped her pacing and walked over to him, her face a picture of vivid anger; mouth compressed in a flat thin line. "If there is no hope," she hissed, "then why the hell did you bring me here?" Her voice rising in rage. "Why couldn't you leave me alone and let me die? Now I am faced with this, this, um, this knowledge," she screamed at him. Screaming obscenities, as the pain finally shattered all her tenuous control, and splattered out, covering both of them in its seething rage. "Why? Why me? Why did he do it? If you are so powerful that you can control time, why didn't you protect me!" she lashed out at him, as finally, the abscess from many years past, burst. Punching, slapping at the Time Weaver, she took all her rage out on him as he just sat there. The putrid anger, her physical beating with the shock waves of each impact being absorbed, was accepted and drawn into his own self.

Slow tears slipped from his eyes, furrowing down his cheeks and melting into his beard.

Melissa's blows abruptly stopped as she fell onto the ground, curled into herself. "God! Why?! Why did he have to do that?" A wailing perplexity of broken trust. The torment of distorted and abused love.

Debased and corrupted humanity, demanding its release on a small child. Gulping, body shaking sobs, she slipped over the edge into the blackness of despair. Security and love sucked through the tear in the fabric of time. Memories flooding, overwhelming and threatening to drown her.

Time Weaver waited silently, then he blew in her direction, speaking quietly, "The North Wind has awakened, come South Wind, blow on this garden that its fragrance may spread everywhere."

A soft wind came from the south, its almost physical presence wrapping around Melissa, warmth swaddling her and building a ladder called hope.

Protected within the warm embrace of his breath, Melissa gradually grew quieter, until her sobs finally hiccupped to a stop.

Time Weaver sang over her:

Lay down in peace and sleep

I only make you to dwell in safety.

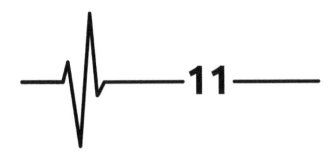

James stirred in his sleep and became aware of a soft, warm body nestled against him. "Mel," he muttered with his sleep-thick mouth.

Stretching he reached over for his wife, suddenly rigidly awake, sitting up with the realisation of pending loss. The soft, warm body shot off him and stood indignantly eyeing him from the end of the bed, tail swishing in annoyance.

"Oh, Oscar. Sorry, mate." He stared in consternation at his pillow, noting the damp patches, thinking, *Not dribble then*. He wiped at his cheeks, noting the salty rivulets where he had cried in his sleep. "Oh, Mel! Please be ok, Mel." Getting out of bed, he stumbled into the bathroom for his morning ablutions. Peering in the mirror, and stroking at the whiskers growing on his chin. "I suppose I should shave," he told Oscar. "Just how in God's name did we come to be in this position, Oscar? Do you know?"

Despair settled again on him. "Fudge! NO!! My phone. I haven't checked it." Bumbling in panicked haste back to the bed, he looked at the screen staring back at him. No message. No link of hope but also no news of sorrow. He went back to the bathroom to finish his shave and wash before heading downstairs, cell phone firmly in hand.

The cat followed, racing him to the kitchen, demanding breakfast. James fed the cat, made coffee and toast and sat idly, staring into nothing. His toast tasted of nothing and the coffee, usually such a rich aroma, felt absent.

He took a deep breath in and huffed it out, closing his eyes against the prickle of tears. *Get it together, James, you can't let the kids see you like this.* He picked Mel's phone up and scrolled through her contacts, looking for Beth Elliot. There, under Beth El. Taking another deep breath, he pressed 'call' and listened as the phone rang.

"Hello," Beth answered.

"Beth, it's James. I'm at home, so I should come around and see you and the kids."

"Oh, James. How is Melissa? We have been praying, and have been asking our prayer group to also pray for you all. Ben and Alex are ok. They are obviously worried about their Mummy, but they can stay here as long as you need them to."

PRAY! thought James. *More prayer stuff! What is this junk!* "uh, ok, thanks. I'll come and see the kids now if it's ok? Do you need me to bring them some clean clothes?"

"It's ok. They fit our kid's clothes, so we are making do. Just come over when you want to. I guess you will be going back to the hospital soon. Tell you what, come over in about ten minutes and I'll make some coffee. Once the kids have seen you, they will be happy to go and play, then Paul, you and I can sit and catch up with what's happening."

As he hung up, James wondered what on earth was happening. First, the conversation about Amy praying, and then his promise to God to go to church, and now Beth? As he bent to stroke Oscar, he picked up his cell phone and the keys. "Time to see the kidlets Oscar. You will be missing them." Checking the front door was locked behind him, he walked dejectedly down the path, straightening and trying to appear confident and happy as he neared Paul & Beth's house. Trying to be strong for Ben and Alex.

"Daddy! Daddy!" Alex came running down the path and flung herself into his arms. "Daddy?" she looked very seriously at him. His heart started to race, wondering what she was going to say, how he would answer her questions. How to tell the truth without causing unnecessary grief or crushing her tiny six-year-old heart? Ben was waiting at the door, watching them, his face cautious. James caught him into a hug, feeling the vibrant life of his children flow through him. Squeezing his eyes tight, he fought against the tears threatening to spill.

"Dad," his nine-year-old son spoke in such a grown-up manner. "Dad, we have been praying for Mum, and Jesus told me she will be ok. He told me not to worry because He has her safe."

What the hell! James thought, his face showing his perplexity. *What have these people been teaching my kids!* "Um, that's great son," he said, messing Ben's hair. His eyes searched Beth's, querying.

"We have all been praying for Ben and Alex's Mummy, haven't we, kids? And Jesus really has spoken to Ben." She put an arm around Ben's shoulders and gave him a quick squeezy hug. "This boy is such a warrior." Clapping her hands, she spoke loudly, "OK kids, go and play now, so the adults can have their coffee in peace. Come on in, James," Beth smiled at him kindly, and he followed her into the house.

Paul stood up, and when James reached out to shake his hand, he was grabbed into a bear hug. As Paul hugged him, James felt his brittle defences crumbling, his shoulders shaking as great gulping sobs tore from his heart, ached out of his throat and gave voice with his mouth. He felt tissues being pressed into his hand, and broke away from Paul. "Sorry, I'm sorry. I don't usually act like this."

"Hey, James, It's ok. You are in the middle of a tremendously hard battle, my friend. We are here for you, ok? Don't worry about showing your emotions. You are safe with us." Paul released James and sat down.

He felt a kindly hand on his shoulder and looked up through the haze of tears at Beth handing him a cup of coffee. "Thank you, " he croaked and crumpled into the closest chair. "Thank you," he said again, looking at the tissues in his hand, blowing his nose and wiping the snot off his top lip.

Beth and Paul sat quietly, allowing peace to envelop James and giving him time to recover his equilibrium. He sat there, hands between his legs, nervously fidgeting with the soaked tissues.

"So, how is she, James?" Beth sipped her coffee.

"When I left the hospital at about one this morning, they were taking her for a C.A.T. scan, to see if," he stopped, his voice catching and took a few deep breaths before being able to continue. "To see if there is any brain function." He looked from Beth to Paul with hollow eyes.

"That would be really hard to hear," Paul said in a quiet, measured voice. "However, as you have heard, we have been praying, and I believe that the Lord God has a great purpose in this. I believe you are going to be surprised." Paul watched James, seeing him struggle to remain calm, knowing he had no faith in God.

Sitting in the neighbour's lounge room, hearing of strange concepts from them, but also that certainty in Ben's voice. He had absolutely known! As James sat struggling with all the bombardment of thoughts, a small quiet voice spoke into his mind *'remember the promise you made me'*. Yes, he had made a bargain with God, but he hadn't really believed that God would listen to him, much less answer. "Thank you. Mel's sister Amy has also been praying, and we aren't religious people, but I guess all good vibes and energy can't harm, can it?" He finished his coffee and carefully putting the mug down, he stood up. "I need to go and see the kids and go back to the hospital. Maybe she will be waking up?" The hope, palpable in the question.

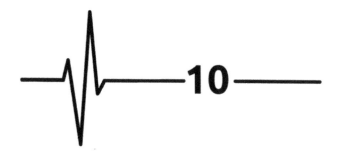

10

There was no alcohol in this place, nothing that would be the placebo she wanted. In the usual way of her life after a meltdown, Melissa would have reached for the wine, masking the pain. Nothing here to bring temporary solace. Nothing to hide behind.

Slowly she sat up and wiped her cheeks. The soft South Wind withdrew, leaving a last flutter of breeze, caressing her hair as it left.

Time Weaver sat cross-legged beside her.

"Now what?" she asked, her voice croakily loud in the small quietude. She felt cut open, as though her heart and thoughts were laying naked between them. All she had believed and treasured lay in shards at her feet. Her eyes pleaded with him. *Do not hurt. Please don't hurt me.* The wrenching fear lay constantly, simmering just underneath, often spilling over the lip of her containment. Panic surfacing while she struggled to subdue it, roiling into unfathomable unreasoning guilt. Wanting to please, wanting to be approved.

"Courage, Dear One," he whispered to her. "Look at me. Always look at me. You will make it if you look at me. When you can't walk, then I will carry you."

With teeth chattering, body shivering anxiety, she looked straight at Time Weaver. Gradually, gradually, the shaking faded. Panic subsided, and fear took a back seat. Hesitantly, she moved her hand, wanting to reach out to him. Still too afraid. Isolation in her deepest seat, being a lifetime habit, her hand fluttered a little. A butterfly longing for release. Afraid of freedom.

In that pause of time, as her hand fluttered, Time Weaver reached out to her, his movement confident and bold to her hesitation. Wrapping her hand in his calloused scarred hand, warmth and love in the gesture.

"Thank you," she said. "Thank you for understanding and not letting me fall into the pit of blackness." She made as though she were going to continue, taking gulps of air. "I've been in that pit before, but you weren't there to help me get out. I thought I had to die, but I was wrong." Melissa could do little more than whisper her confession for the words were being choked as tears ached in her throat.

Those deep brown eyes of his. A rugged face framed by dark curly hair and punctuated with his beard. Not handsome. No. But so desirable. Melissa felt herself being drawn into the acceptance that he wore like a robe.

The aching echo of her broken heart's chambers resonated loudly. Still, Time Weaver held her hand. Not letting go of her.

"May I have a hug?" she asked him, tremulously, fearing rejection.

"I so wanted you to ask me for that," he responded and enveloped her in his arms.

She could hear his heart singing its love to her, rhythmical beats inviting her in. Safe. She had never felt this safe. And the joy! Welling up, every cell of her being pinged with joy. Nerve synapses unfolding into life.

"So, my Melissa," Time Weaver still had hold of Melissa's hand. He pulled her to standing and started swinging their hands, up and down, up and down, then He began to skip, giving her little choice but to skip with him.

She began to giggle. "What are you doing? If you are God, shouldn't you be all, like, you know, all serious?"

He laughed. Laughed so hard he was doubled over. "I so love you, Melissa. Do you know, when I was in Capernaum, my disciples came to me and asked a question. And the answer to that question is the answer to your question. 'Unless you become like a little child, you will never enter the Kingdom of Heaven'. There are enough serious people here without getting all religious in my home."

She ripped her hand out of his. "Stop. Just stop! I am so confused. Here you are saying you are God, but you are joking and laughing. Are you mocking me? I don't get it. Everything I know about church is that it is cold and boring. It is full of rules and do's and don'ts. And I've broken them all. There is no way I can be like a little child. You said yourself that Ken stole my childhood, so how do you expect me to now become like a child again?"

"It's a conundrum, isn't it?" Time Weaver walked back and forth, back and forth. "What is so very simple, man has made into a formidable barrier to knowing me." He spread his arms wide, the scars on his hands very apparent. "But you, Melissa, what about you?"

She stared at him. Joy fading. The ever-present anger taking over yet again. "What about me? Well? WHAT ABOUT ME!" she shouted at him, "According to you, I'm not dead. I stuffed that up as well. And now? Well now, I'm stuck in a place with someone who claims to be God but doesn't act like God. I'm still bloody miserable. I don't want to live, but clearly, I don't want to die either. So, what about me then, GOD!" she spat the last word at him, anger and hatred dripping off each letter.

"Tell me what you think God should be like, then?" Even with her anger, his eyes were twinkling.

"Well, he's um, he's like a really stern grandfather. Someone who is watching to get you if you misbehave. He will zap you to hell if you don't follow all the rules." She crinkled her forehead in thought. "Oh yes, and you aren't allowed fun, you know, party, get drunk, all that stuff." Her face screwed up as she thought of the angry God. Someone she could never trust. Someone vengeful, just waiting for her to make a wrong step.

Making a thoughtful face, Time Weaver nodded. "Ok then, so shall we see if that is the truth?"

"I suppose!" she responded sullenly.

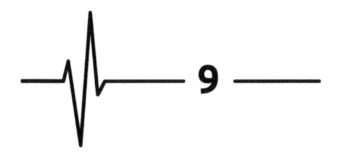

Hospital car parks are a nightmare. James took the ticket as he drove into the park, looking for the first available space. *I wonder how much this will cost?* he thought. *The budget is already strained.*

Finding a park, he quickly got out and locked the car. *It looks like it's going to rain, and I don't have a coat or umbrella. Matches my mood, I guess!* James strode across the car park to the main entrance and took the elevator to the ICU unit. Checking his watch, he was startled to see that it had only been 16 hours since he had first found Melissa. He felt as though it had been a lifetime of existing in a black nightmare.

Stopping at the cafe by the ICU unit for a coffee to go, he paused. What will I find? What will the outcome of the C.A.T. scan be? Will I still have a wife, or will there only be a vegetable? Will she even survive? Taking a gulp of his coffee, which burnt his mouth, he tried to appear confident as he waited to be allowed into the unit.

The doors swung open, and softly now, he walked towards Mel's cubicle. Trepidation walked with him, fear an icy companion to his left. Closing his eyes briefly, before sliding the curtain across, anxiety causing the hair follicles on his head to tighten as the muscles contracted.

The nurse looked up and smiled as he walked in. "Hi", he said. "I'm James, Mel's husband," and stood uncertainly. Did he want to find out bad news first, or go and kiss Melissa and remain ignorant of her condition? "Um, did she have the C.A.T. scan?" he chose the hard option, trying to appear staunch, being brave.

"She has remained stable through the night. The doctors will be doing rounds soon, and you will be told about the results of the scan then," the nurse said, as she looked at him compassionately, then turned her attention back to the reports and monitors, leaving James to go to Melissa.

He leaned over the bed and kissed her. On the forehead. On the cheek. Unable to kiss her mouth, which was held firm by the intubation equipment. Taking her hand, he kissed that too. "Hi, Honey. I'm sorry I was away so long. I needed to sleep and go to see Ben and Alex." He stroked her hand, stroked her hair, looking at the monitors again; watching for any change from last night. Oh, that he could read and understand what they said.

"Mel, can you hear me? Please let me know you can hear me." Despairing, he let his head drop onto the bed, nestled between her shoulder and neck. Comfort just in that. Even her own smell had changed. Only a chemical, hospital, smell. The curtains rustled, and he sat up as the doctor and his entourage came in.

"Female, aged 40, currently in a Propofol-induced coma following intentional drug overdose of a nonbenzodiazepine and alcohol. C.A.T. scan results to hand." The consultant addressed the more junior doctors.

Turning his attention to James, he said, "Mr. Stuart, the C.A.T. scan results showed good brain wave function. However, we will not know the extent of the damage until we bring Melissa out of the coma, in about eight hours." The consultant looked carefully to ensure James understood what was being said. He went through the routine of checking her eyes and reflexes, and then nodding to James, left the room with the group following behind like a school of obedient children.

Eight hours! James thought. "Just eight hours, honey. Did you hear that? Then it will all be ok again," he told Melissa.

"Mr. Stuart?" A woman came into Melissa's room. She put her hand out to shake James' hand. "Mr. Stuart, my name is Dr. Norris. I'm a psychologist from the psych liaison team. In situations such as this, we are here to ensure the whole family feels safe and supported."

"Uhh. Hi." James extended his hand to shake hers. *More psychobabble stuff?* he thought.

"You have two children?"

James nodded. "Yes, Ben and Alex."

"Are they aware of Melissa's overdose?"

"No, they just know that Mummy is sick in hospital. They are with a neighbour who has children the same age. They know them really well."

"Oh, That's really good," she said, "What about spiritual support? Do you have a community around you for support?"

James stared at her. *What is with all this God stuff,* he thought. *Amy, Beth, the kids praying now.* "Um, no," he replied, "we don't go to any church. My sister-in-law is religious, so if we need help in that direction, we can ask her."

Dr. Norris nodded to James and wrote in her notes. "Ok, Thank you for your time. This is my card, and if you need someone to talk to, the office can direct you. We are here to assist. Times such as these are very traumatic and can raise many issues and questions. There is a Spiritual Centre or Chapel available in the hospital if you need it."

"Thanks. I appreciate your time." James looked at her card and then put it in his wallet.

She bustled off, leaving James alone with Melissa, under the vigilant care of the ICU nurse.

He stood up and yawned, stretching restlessly. Prowling around the room, looking at anything that might be interesting. Three walls and a curtain, no window. *I wish I'd brought a book or even a woman's magazine. I'm bored,* he thought. *Maybe I will get some lunch, and there might be a magazine or something in the shop downstairs. Even check Facebook. Anything, so I won't be so bored.* "I think I'll go and get some lunch now," he said to the ICU nurse. "Please make sure you phone me if anything changes." He looked at her pleadingly, as he exited the curtained room.

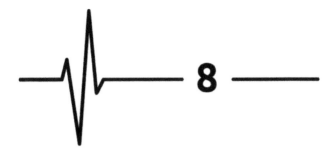

8

"You saw what happened at the dawn of time, Melissa. How mankind chose to rebel, and in so doing, caused their own destruction. But what is the backstory to that? Why did it happen?"

"Mmm-Mmm," she shrugged her shoulders.

He smiled at her. "OK, let's find out, then, shall we?" Time Weaver spoke two words, commanding: "Truth. Come!" The atmosphere shook.

The place where they stood changed. She was no longer in the insubstantial, ethereal place. Time Weaver had gone.

She was standing at the back of what appeared to be a courtroom. An angel was by her. *How do I know it's an angel?* Thoughts were buzzing wildly through her head. If being with Time Weaver before had felt strange, this was even more bizarre; completely outside her sphere of reference. "What's happening?" she whispered to the angel.

"The Most High God wants you to know the truth. In knowing the truth, you will be set free."

She looked at the angel. He was incredibly beautiful. Really tall, strong, and so masculine. And that hair! What she would do for that hair. It fell in glistening waves down his back, and the only word she could find, to describe the colour, was champagne. It wasn't blonde, and it wasn't red. It wasn't silver but had all of those hues. Then she looked at him again, peering behind his back. "Where are your wings? I thought angels had wings."

The angel grinned at her. "Not all angels have wings. We don't need them to move through time and eternity."

"OK then," she looked at him sceptically. "So, just where are we, then?" Melissa queried. She was looking around. There were a vast number of angels and strange creatures gathered. A group of them were herded together and being guarded by angels in full armour, with swords ready for action. The atmosphere was tense, filled with fear by the ones under guard, and anger from the others. The murmuring was sombre and strained. There was something else too, something she could feel but had no words for. *Fear? No, not fear but like fear.* She could not put a word to it.

The angel put a hand on her arm. His face was grave. "We are in the High Court of Heaven. There has never been an open session held here before. This is what the Son wants you to see."

Before Melissa could query who the 'Son' was, there came a sudden shuffling announcing something imminent. Double doors, HUGE doors swung open. Two angels, obviously high ranking, strode into the courtroom and made their way to the front. The assembly parted way to allow them through, heads bowing respectfully.

"The dark one, that looks like an Indian, is the Archangel Michael. He is Commander of Heaven's warrior angels." He pointed at the other one, who stood tall and had the appearance of gold, and said "And that one is Gabriel. Gabriel is also an archangel, and stands in the presence of the Lord God. Whenever Gabriel goes out from the Presence Chamber, you can expect to see change. He is the message bearer, the one who stands and decrees."

Twenty Four elderly men walked in and seated themselves before the judge's bench. The entire assembly of angels bowed to them.

"These are the Twenty Four Elders. They may look old, but that is the title they wear. They are as vigorous and young as the rest of us. You will notice that whichever section of Heaven we are from, then that is the appearance we take." The angel scanned the room. "Oh, and no one here can see you or me. The Lord God, the Son and the Spirit of God are the only others who know you are here. My brothers have simply been told that I am on assignment."

"So, I'm invisible, then?" That was such a cool thing to know. If only she could take the invisibility cloak back with her! HA!

And then the atmosphere changed. That fear-feeling she could not aptly describe, intensified. All her skin prickled, the weight of who she really was, became very heavy. There was a palpable change in atmosphere and every being suddenly bowed as deeply as possible; some prostrating themselves on the floor. She herself, felt forced to her knees by that ineffable, indefinable atmosphere. Even the prisoners bowed low and fell to their knees.

There was silence in Heaven.

How she knew who the three beings, who simply appeared, were, she didn't understand. But, as they took their place at the judge's bench, she knew she was in the presence of God and that the fear she had felt, truly was fear. It was the fear and respect of Almighty God, and she was in His presence. Her body was shaking, and all she had ever thought good and right, everything she had believed or not believed, suddenly appeared as rubble.

Gabriel stepped forward. He had in his hands a scroll, which he unrolled. In a voice of gravel, he started to read. "Charges of treason are brought before this court. That Lucifer, the Cherub who covered the throne of God, together with one-third of the Angels, did instigate and bring war to Heaven. That Lucifer, you did desire and plot to overthrow the righteous government of Heaven and to depose the Lord God from His rightful place. Furthermore, you did plot to deceive mankind and thus destroy the new creation." His words fell into the silence as stones, landing heavily.

Melissa looked at the angels. It was frightening. Their faces shadowed grief, followed by anger and bewilderment.

Gabriel was speaking again. "Do you deny these charges, Lucifer?"

The most beautiful being Melissa had ever seen stepped toward Gabriel. "I am the angel who covers. It is my right to be heard in this court and tried fairly. By the laws that the Lord God governs by, I demand my rights. My right is that this puny mankind chose to follow me. I am now their king, and I own them and this creation called earth. I own the galaxies, the universes and all in them. I am their king, and I demand these laws be recognised." And he stepped back.

Waves of murmuring swept across the angelic gathering. The angels on trial looked smug. Lucifer held his head high, proud and haughty, as he waited on the decision of the judges.

Oh, no! Melissa thought. She remembered what Time Weaver had shown her. That beautiful, strange-looking creature that duped Eve, and there it was, standing next to the one called Lucifer. She looked at the Judges. Their faces were implacable.

The Lord God raised His right hand. There was an instant stillness. "Lucifer speaks correctly. By my own laws, mankind has given themselves into his hands. He now owns the new creation, earth, and mankind.

Horrified gasps fractured the air.

"However," God continued, and the whispering abated. "However! By my own laws, you are correct, Lucifer, but there is a higher law, which supersedes that." He paused, giving time for that statement to be absorbed. "Before I created you Lucifer, I knew what you would do. Before you were created BY ME," he roared. "I put the laws in place."

Consternation rattled the condemned angels. Whispers amongst the leaders.

Leaning over the judge's bench, the Lord glared at Lucifer. "Yes. The higher law states; If there is one who is willing to give himself and stand in the place of man, then and only then can mankind be redeemcd."

Lucifer was confounded. The group around him drew back, imperceptibly.

The Lord continued. "As mankind is human flesh and blood, then only a perfect, pure and unblemished sacrifice in human form can ever cover and bring salvation to man and to earth. Blood to blood, flesh to flesh." The Lord God stared hard at Lucifer, who was previously known as the 'one who covers'. "Is there such a one present?"

Melissa clutched frantically at the angel with her. "Tell me this is not happening," she said, "Are they going to kill someone?"

The angel looked at her. "It is the only way to redeem this creation. They gave themselves willingly to Lucifer. They are flesh and blood, and the only way to ransom them is for another human being, who is completely perfect and carries no sin, to die on their behalf. Someone who carries the same flesh and blood DNA as mankind, so that the sinless one will cover over the sin of mankind." He looked worried. "There is no such being. Man is lost forever to Lucifer."

Feeling her legs giving way under her at the horror she was witnessing, Melissa slowly sank to the floor.

The Judge, the Lord God, spoke again. "I call once more. Is there such a one present? One who bears the same flesh and blood as mankind?"

Lucifer looked smug. He looked arrogant and supremely pleased with himself. The angels and creatures around him started patting each other on the back, congratulating one another on their massive win. For win it was. They had stung God in His heart, destroyed what He had held so precious, and now it was theirs to do with as they wanted.

A wave of disturbance from the shuffling of feet was coming from the Judges Bench. Melissa watched as Time Weaver stood up. "I am he. I am the Lamb. I am the sacrifice, and I will redeem this world." Waves of rainbows emanated from around Him. Power flexed and rippled forth.

Lucifer screamed out in anger. "You can't do that! That is against your own laws." He charged towards the Judges while Michael and other warriors unsheathed their swords, blocking his access.

"Get back, Lucifer," Michael growled, his face shadowed with intense anger.

Fixing Lucifer with an unrelenting, intractable look, Time Weaver answered him, "I am bound by my Father's laws, and I have decreed that I will redeem what you stole. I am the Lamb whom you have slain since the beginning of this earth." And he sat back down.

Melissa sat with her mouth open, a keening wail escaped, with tears of distress and horror pouring from her, running down her cheeks and dropping onto the floor. A strange thing happened each time a tear hit the ground; it turned into a precious stone. "What is this?" she cried to the angel.

"Oh! Yes, that. Every time one of mankind cries righteous tears, they are caught and held in a crystal bottle, awaiting the time for release. Precious in the sight of the Lord, are their tears."

Her mouth formed into an 'O' of surprise. Her former concept of God was being shattered. "But what is going to happen? They can't do that to Time Weaver. He is so beautiful. He is perfect. They can't kill him!"

The angel reached out and touched her. Melissa fell into a deep sleep.

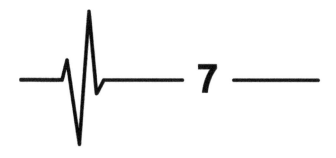

7

She awoke to being knocked around on all sides as a great stream of people hurried about, seemingly without even noticing her. A brawling, bustling crowd. There were great marble pillars holding up a magnificent portico, which was attached to an equally magnificent building. Self-important people in sumptuous robes were hurrying. She had no idea where she was or what was happening.

The early morning sky, which was streaked with pink, heralded a beautiful spring day. There should be life in the atmosphere, but all she could feel was foreboding. A rooster crowed. She looked around her and saw a group. Soldiers. Guarding a prisoner. A hand touched and held her arm, and she whirled around. It was the angel who had been with her in the courtroom. "It's time," he said.

"What? Time for what? Where am I?" Melissa struggled against the Angel's hold on her arm.

"It is time to see this earth being redeemed from Lucifer." The angel pulled her through the crowds, right to the front where they saw Time Weaver, bound to a post and completely naked. A Roman soldier stood near him, holding a whip.

Melissa stopped in shock. Her stomach heaved as her heart raced and pounded, and her breath came in little gasps. Her entire focus was on the whip, as the soldier held the wooden handle, with the three leather thongs draping across the ground. Each time he moved, the pieces of ragged metal embedded into each strand, scraped across the ground.

A man who appeared to be of great importance was in earnest conversation with men in priestly robes. He looked at them with distaste and called a slave to bring a basin of water. Washing his hands in the water, he cried in a loud voice, "I find no fault in this man, however, because he is a Jew, and according to your laws, let him be flogged." Nodding to the soldier, the man of importance sat down, looking on impassively.

"No one can see you or hear you, except Time Weaver. You are here to see just what he did for you." The angel's face contorted in compassion.

The soldier raised the whip. Melissa cringed. He lowered it again, laughing as some other soldiers came across the paved yard, carrying a crown made of thorns. Thorns as long as her thumb. Cruelly, they jammed it onto Time Weaver's head, ensuring the thorns went right into his flesh. Melissa gasped. "King, are you?" they taunted him, slapping him across the face. They walked away, laughing mockingly.

Time Weaver turned and looked straight at Melissa. Into her mind flooded words of undying love and forgiveness. You are precious. If you were the only one on this earth, I would still endure this so you could live with us forever. I love you, Melissa. I love you. I forgive you. I am doing this for you.

Raising the whip again, the soldier brought it down.

Down it struck. First lash. The three thongs landing viciously across Time Weaver's shoulders. He jerked but was silent. Still looking at Melissa. Words sparked off each thong as they landed: *lies, deceit, slander, gossip, vile accusations.*

Down came the whip again, curling around Time Weaver's back and thudding into his ribs. Ruby blots of blood following the lash marks. CRACK, as his ribs were assaulted. *Murder, theft, envy, greed, corruption, abandonment, jealousy, betrayal,* flowed from the end of the jagged metal, as it ripped open his back.

Melissa's knees buckled, but the angel held her upright.

Down came the leather and metal. His flesh was broken open. *Adultery, fornication, perversion, drunkenness, idolatry* flowed from his broken back.

Again, and again. Again, and again. Each time worse than the other, exposing his inner organs, veins, and arteries, right down to his bowels and ripping around to his front lacerating his chest, laying it open. Words continuing to pour off the end of the whip. *Witchcraft, idolatry, pride, lust, rebellion, selfishness.* Every evil thought and deed done by mankind.

Down it came. Disease, poverty, famine, despair, incest, abortion.

Down it came. Sickness, fear, religious control, war, rape, spells, hexes

Down it came. Ripping across his head and face, pulling out his beard and hair. Thirty-eight times. Down it came. Every bone in his back and head exposed.

Every wrong thing Melissa had ever done or thought, was laid bare with each lash of that whip, as it cried out her sin and shame.

Down it came for the thirty-ninth time. The cruel strands wrapping around and ripping apart his groin.

Even as the flagellum broke open, and even as it destroyed, a song was released. *By these stripes, you are healed. Freedom, joy, healing, restoration*, it rang out into the atmosphere. *Life, peace, hope, salvation, deliverance.* His blood dripped onto the cobblestones, which hummed as they received to themselves, his very life.

His brokenness sang a song of freedom and healing.

For He brings healing, healing to you.

The notes danced over to Melissa, while the melody sang; going in through her ears, rejoicing down into her heart. The tune danced inside her.

For he brings healing, healing to you.

She started to hum to the melody, a subtle change in the words.

For he brings healing, healing to me.

The soldier panted, his work in the beating done. His tunic spattered with Time Weaver's blood and flesh, each piece singing a refrain.

'Kingdom. The kingdom. Kingdom. Messiah has come,'

resounded in harmony.

So bloody and beaten in its scourging, His body unable to support itself, he lay in his own gore. Time Weaver could no longer stand. Humiliation clothing him like a robe. Thus, the King of all Heaven, the Creator of the universe, King of Kings, Lord of Lords, lay beaten and bloodily broken. No golden robes or crowns.

Suddenly, Melissa started to understand. "As mankind is human flesh and blood, then only a perfect, pure and unblemished sacrifice in human form, can ever cover and bring salvation to man and to earth. Blood to blood, flesh to flesh." echoed through her mind, setting up a kettle-drum beat. Blood to blood, flesh to flesh, blood to blood, flesh to flesh.

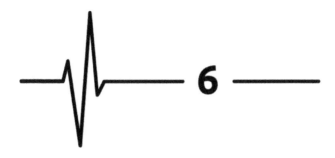

6

"Come now. We have to go," the angel interrupted Melissa's thoughts.

She looked about and noticed a massive piece of wood was being foisted onto Time Weaver's broken back. He cried out, staggering in torment as that rough-sawn log dug into the raw flesh and juddered on his exposed spine. He staggered over the cobbles, dragging the forty-five-kilo log behind him. And fell. On his knees, already ripped open where the lash had bitten and shredded. The soldiers kicked him, swearing, but his endurance was gone. He could not get up.

Even in his agonising pain, he turned and looked at Melissa and into her heart came;

I bring healing. Healing for you. Even if you were the only one Melissa, I would still endure this.

I take this onto myself willingly, just for you. For you, I accept this cross. Don't ever take your eyes off me.

A soldier scanned the gathered crowd and pointed at a man who had been standing watching what was happening. "Here. You. Carry it." He was pushed into place behind Time Weaver, where the beam was shoved onto his back. So, Time Weaver shakily made his way on, the 1700 staggering paces to Golgotha, falling often.

A woman was following him, her face covered in distress, and each time he fell, she would dart out and gently help him up. The soldiers pushed her out of the way, swearing at her. She fell backwards but scrambled up quickly, so as not to get left behind, staying as close as she could.

Through the streets of Jerusalem, from the stone pavement in front of Herod's palace, the way of suffering led Time Weaver inexorably on. Past the tower of David near the Jaffa gate, out of the Porta Esquilina, outside the city walls.

The sun was directly overhead. Crowded streets thinned as women left the markets and made their way home to prepare for Passover. Still, Time Weaver agonisingly journeyed through the narrow lanes; the stranger carrying his cross for him, closer and closer to the place of the skull.

6

Melissa and the Angel followed in silence. Standing a way off, they watched as the procession stopped. The soldiers took the cross beam off the stranger and shoved him to one side. He was obviously of no further use to them.

Kicking the cross beam into position, Time Weaver was then pushed back, so he fell, torn and bloody shoulders hit hard against the beam, and his head hit cruelly against the sun-packed ground. His cries of anguish fractured through Melissa's mind.

"Shut up!" A soldier kicked him again, as he dragged one of Time Weaver's arms across the wood, tying it in place at the wrist and then doing the same with the other arm. Another soldier followed the pattern, but with a mallet and large iron nails, as long as a man's hand, which he hammered straight through Time Weaver's palms and into the wood. His screams ripped into the onlookers, some who mocked and some who cried.

Melissa could no longer stand. The Angel supported her as she fell heavily onto her knees. A wraith of horror spiralled around her. Time Weaver turned his head to her. '*I bring healing. Healing for you. Even if you were the only one, Melissa, I would still endure this. Don't ever take your eyes off me,*' His words settled over her, speaking into her mind, her heart.

Looping ropes through the two ends of the patibulum, the soldiers then started to drag Time Weaver and his log across the ground, where his open wounds tore on the stony ground. Heaving the man and cross beam up to the upright piece, they were slotted into the notch and secured in place. His open wounds were littered with wood splinters. More huge nails hammered his feet, one across the other, onto the upright beam.

Time Weaver hung there, between heaven and earth. Being pulled down toward the earth, compressed his lungs so he couldn't breathe. In pushing up to be able to breathe, the nails tore his feet more, and whichever way he pushed or relaxed, shards of wood drove into his exposed, internal organs. His spine grated against the hardened grain. Down, to gain freedom from agony tearing at his feet. Up, to be able to breathe. Roughness ripping, torment never giving way.

The Angel bowed his head.

Of all that Melissa had learned about Time Weaver, this was the furthest away from what she could have imagined. The beautiful, loving heart, kindness, and joy were still there. But the power and authority seemed to be in abeyance. Why couldn't He just command and the angels would come and rescue Him? If He was God, why didn't He just zap all these people?

She looked up, as a shadow appeared to momentarily darken the brilliant day, but sceing nothing, looked back at Time Weaver, the crowd, the woman who had followed Him all the way.

Another shadow seemed to dim the spring light, and the Angel suddenly became very tense and alert, scanning the sky.

"I wasn't imagining it," Melissa remarked to herself, for overhead was gathering a horde of the ugliest beings she had never hoped to see.

"They were my brothers," the Angel said to her, "These are the ones you saw in the judgment hall."

"But they were so beautiful," Melissa protested, "These are unbelievably ugly!"

"Yes, they are. They carry in their very bodies and faces, the thing that they hold in their hearts - hatred." The Angel's face contorted in momentary sadness.

The sky grew darker and darker. Those gathered to watch the crucifixions, looked up in consternation, but couldn't see any reason for the developing darkness.

Mocking laughter resounded overhead. Insults poured from the mouths of the fallen angels.

And then.

Then they produced large buckets, and from these buckets, they poured more darkness. Evil, vile creatures pouring buckets of filth onto the purest person Melissa had ever known.

Bucket after bucket after bucket. Filth, worse than excrement, dripped down and flowed into his wounds.

"There!" she shouted at her companion Angel. "Look." She watched as an evil one poured out a bucket labelled murder. Man-like wraith forms fell screaming onto Time Weaver, stabbing him with knives, shooting him with guns, strangulation and all kinds of horror, whose sole aim was to kill. Suicide joined them, along with drug addiction, alcoholism. All manner of self-destruction.

Laughing maniacally, other creatures poured out their buckets.

"It is time," her Angel said. "This is what you are here for. Look."

She looked up and saw some huge demonic beings with their buckets. They tipped them over, and the contents leapt onto Time Weaver. Every vile thing that Ken had ever done to her, they did to Time Weaver. All the manipulation and lies, all the filth and coercion. All the physical acts he had done to her, they did to Him.

6

Bucket, after bucket, after bucket, pouring out as unadulterated evil. So great was the company of evil ones that the sky was dark. Total darkness in the middle of the afternoon.

He writhed under the torment, but out of Him poured forgiveness. His blood dripped down and covered the world under that cross.

She screamed.

Screamed. Screamed. Screamed.

Her Angel touched her. "It's time to go. You have seen what He wanted you to witness."

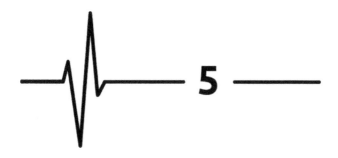

5

Pushing his lunch away, James answered the cell phone call. Unknown number. "Hello." The voice came through, static distorting the connection. He stood up, so as to find a better signal, and knocked his coffee, slopping it onto the table. "ah, fudge," he muttered, "No, sorry, not to you," he told the caller. "I just knocked my coffee." Listening carefully, he repeated what the caller said. "OK, so 4.30 pm in the consultation room. Yes, I can find it. Thank you."

Cutting the call off, he slumped back down in the cafe chair. His heart was ramming out of his chest. Reflexively, he looked at his watch. Two o'clock. Two and a half hours to kill. *Wonder if I have time to get back to the kids for an hour or so?* He mulled over the options in his mind, and then making a decision, drank the rest of the coffee, took another bite out of his sandwich, and headed for the car park.

While it wasn't far to drive home, the traffic was starting to build. It might be Saturday, but the cars never seemed to stop. *Maybe it's not such a good idea to go home, after all*, he thought, and changing his plan, drove towards the local park.

This is the loneliest time of my life. The waiting is unbearable. He found a park bench and sat, hoping no one would want to interrupt his self-imposed isolation.

The birds flitted from tree to tree, looking for insects. The insects flitted from flower to flower, branches, twigs, and leaves. Fish plopped, breaking the surface of the small lake in the park, grabbing at the insects flying over the water, as the birds, in turn, grabbed at the insects.

What perfect coordination, he thought. Everything in its right place, in perfect balance. Until man wrecks it, that is.

One word: 'balance' came into his mind. 'perfect balance.' Yes, he thought, I find it hard to believe this all came from an amoeba, crawling out of the primordial soup, or even a big bang. Surely, there is design behind this? Isn't that what science is saying now? Everything in perfect union?

Suddenly, he stopped his meandering thoughts. "NO," he said out loud, startling the sparrow that had been busy looking for grubs. An elderly man stopped and looked at him.

"Did you say something?" he asked.

"Uh, no, just thinking out loud." James was embarrassed.

"Aye well, sometimes it's the only way to make sense of life, isn't it?" The old man ambled over to James and sat down next to him. "When my wife was dying, I was angry. She was too young. Left me with teenage children and I didn't know what to do with them. I told God what I thought of him, then." He stopped and chuckled. "Didn't do me much good. You can't argue with the Creator." The man smiled ruefully. "No, Sir," he shook his head. "You can't argue with the Creator."

He sighed, "Isn't this all so beautiful?" He waved his hand at the peaceful scene before them. "So perfect its balance."

The two men sat together in silent contemplation.

There is no way he could have known about Mel! James cast the man sideways glances. No, he couldn't have known.

"Whatever it is that you are troubled about young man, know this. There is a God who died for you. He really does care. "The old man heaved himself off the park bench and shuffled off.

James stared after him. *How did he know?! Was this coincidence?* He checked his watch. "Better get back to the hospital," he said, smiling self-consciously, as two young girls looked at him talking to himself. "Weirdo James," he muttered.

He allowed his thoughts to wander where they wanted as he drove to the hospital and found a park. The thoughts wafted around through that particular hospital smell. Free reign as he passed by the cafe on the ground floor. Uninterrupted reverie as he walked by the sign that said 'chapel.'

He stopped. Chapel.

Hesitantly, he pushed the door open. It was empty. A seat off to the right beckoned him, and he sat there in the dim quiet. Trying desperately to quiet his mind's deliberation, he started to take each piece apart. Mel's sister Amy had been talking about God-stuff for a long time. It didn't make sense. Beth and Paul praying. Ben saying that he had heard Jesus. The psych worker. The random man in the park. Around and around and around, until finally James looked at his watch and was startled to see it was 4:15. He had better hurry to the consultant's appointment.

Condition normal, James thought. The consultant was late. James sat waiting, flicking through magazines, trying to make sense of the whole mess.

Finally. The Doctor came rushing in. "Good. You are here. Come in." James followed him into his office, taking a seat on the other side of the desk.

Steepling his hands, the Doctor looked at James for just a second and then reached for a file. "I've reviewed Melissa's file and examined her. The C.A.T. scan showed what appears to be satisfactory brain function. However," and as he said that, he looked gravely at James. "As I said last night, until she comes out of the coma, we will not know the full extent of the damage." He paused. It was obviously as difficult for the Doctor, as it was for James. "Mr. Stuart. You have to be prepared that your wife may never properly regain consciousness, and if that is the case, then she will need around-the-clock care."

Shock hit James.

"Now, if she needs permanent care," the doctor continued, "there is also a high chance that she will be unable to breathe on her own. We won't know until we remove the life support. Mr. Stuart, do you have any idea why your wife tried to take her own life?"

If only he'd listened. If only he'd listened, beat incessantly through his mind. "Yes. She'd been having counselling for child sex abuse. She couldn't handle it anymore."

"Don't blame yourself." The Doctor looked at him, kindly. "It is a very hard thing to heal from. Because the overdose was intentional, she will be transferred to a mental health unit for evaluation." Seeing the look of shock on James' face, he reassured him. "It's usually only a 72-hour assessment, during which time the psychiatrist will evaluate her needs.

"When do you plan to remove the breathing thing?" James' voice sounded to him as though it was in a cave, dull and hushed.

The consultant looked at his watch. "It's 5 pm now. I will aim for around 7.30pm. It's not a good idea that you watch. We will let you into the room as soon as we can. Right now, I suggest you go home. Get something to eat and come back, say at 8 pm."

Nodding dumbly, James rose from the chair. No thought, except of Melissa. Round the clock care. Unable to breathe.

Pausing at the door to nod again and thank the Doctor, he left.

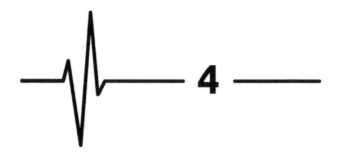

4

With a shuddering gasp, Melissa sat up. "Have I been asleep?" Swiping at her eyes and looking around, she saw she was back in that insubstantial place. "I've had the most awful nightmare," she said. She touched her cheeks. They were wet with tears. "I dreamed such awful things were done to you. Oh, God!"

Time Weaver looked at her, such love palpable on his face. "It's time for the rest of the truth now, Melissa." He said, holding his hand out and pulling her up. "I've been making a tapestry."

Melissa stood up. Closing her eyes for a moment, took a couple of deep, shaky breaths. "OK. It's only a dream. Right, then. Show me what you've been making." She pushed the nightmare away, and walked over to the loom where Time Weaver had been working.

"I'm weaving the tapestry of your life, my Beloved." Taking his seat at the loom, he started his work again. Click swish, click swish, as the shuttle went back and forth on the loom. He smiled at her while continuing the click swish of his work. "It is unfinished, just as your life is unfinished. I know what I want to weave, and I know what was sung over you when my Father conceived you in his heart."

She looked at him curiously. "What do you mean 'your Father'? You mean God? I thought you *were* God."

He grinned at her. "Confusing, huh?! It's not really, when you get to know us. We are three, but we are one."

The beginning of the tapestry was in brilliant colour. Magnificent, hopeful, colour. As the weaving grew, the colour faded out to muted hues and disintegrated into a lifeless muddy stain. "Well, if that's my life, it doesn't look very pretty. I wouldn't hang that on my wall," she said, as she continued to examine the cloth, then exclaimed, "And there's a big hole in the middle of it! Why have you made it with a hole?"

Pausing his work, he looked intently at her. "That hole is where I belong in your life. Without me in the middle of all you are, there will always be a hole in your life. Nothing else can fit into this hole except me.

You have spun out the threads that form the tapestry of your life. You wove your cloth without me, and this is how it has turned out."

Leaning in closer, she examined the tapestry, touching the beginning of it, where flashes of light wove into luminescent pinks and red. "But what will it look like when it's finished?" she asked him.

"That all depends on whether you allow me to be the centre of your life, or if you continue on without me. The hole in the tapestry will only ever be filled, if you put me there."

She looked puzzled. "I don't understand what that means. How can you be in the centre of my life?"

"Before you were even conceived, the scroll of your life was written. Your design and destiny, the very purpose of your life was called out and recorded. You accepted your scroll before you left our heart. Then, you forgot all about us and continued on down your life's path, alone. We have been at every point, holding hands out to you, but you have chosen not to walk with us. Therefore, the tapestry now being woven, has a hole which destroys the beauty of it, as it is not complete."

Puzzlement written all over her face, she looked at him and looked back at the tapestry. "So, you are saying, that the rest of the tapestry would change, if you were in the middle of it?"

"That's exactly what I'm saying. And furthermore, this horrible patch right in the middle of the tapestry, the muddy part, would also change. I would crown you with a diadem to glorify and adorn you, in place of the worthlessness of your life. I will pour my oil of joy in exchange for your sorrow, so you will rejoice. You will live in praise for the rest of your life, swapping the heaviness you are carrying for my joy. This is the purpose of your life."

Considering this for a while, Melissa wandered around the area, coming back to the tree. Running her hand along the branch they had been sitting on, she turned back to Time Weaver. "But how do I make you the centre of my life? Do you, like, do you get inside me or something? Something 'woo woo' like. Ooky-spooky type stuff? Or is it about going to church?"

Carefully, he put the shuttle aside and stood up. "You have seen the demise of mankind, Melissa. We watched that horror together, and saw how even through millennia of women, you are still tied back to the first woman. DNA following DNA, following DNA, and on and on. Each a part of the other. Did you realise that you were already in your grandmother's ovum, at the time of her birth? And that she passed that same DNA onto your mother, who then passed it onto you? That at the time of your conception, the DNA you had present in your own ovum, was also going to pass onto Alex, and then again onto Alex's daughter?"

"Are you for real? Is that true?!"

"Yes, it is true, and while, of course, we designed it to be that way, science is just catching up with that concept."

"OK, I can accept that," she said, shrugging her shoulders. "It sounds kind of logical. But I want to know, how do I have you in the middle of my life? How does that happen? And if that does happen, does all this sadness just disappear? How do you make four years of hell go away?"

"Remember, Melissa? 'I bring healing. Healing for you. Even if you were the only one, Melissa, I would still endure this. Don't ever take your eyes off me,'"

Bubbling, rushing up in a torrent, a cascade that caused her to stare at him with wide-eyed horror, she saw again the courtroom scene. Time Weaver declaring himself as the lamb. As the one who would give himself as the ultimate sacrifice. Watching him be whipped until he was beyond recognition. Seeing the brutality as he gave himself, willingly, to be executed. Knowing that he could have called on every Angel and they would have obeyed him. But he didn't. He kept telling her, over and over again, *I did it all for you, Melissa*. She looked again at his ugly, scarred hands.

Finally, she understood.

Rigid with horror in dawning realisation, that what he did, all the ghastly things that she had seen in the nightmare, were true.

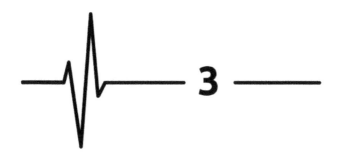

3

"Come," He said. "I have one last thing to show you."

He touched her shoulder. Instantly she recognised her mother's kitchen. She was 12 years old again. Staring about her, the cooker, the cupboards, the table. All exactly the same. The scene of so many encounters of the gross kind. Agonising loss rose up. Four years of her life all converging on this one point; by the refrigerator.

Time Weaver stood close to her. "What happened?" he asked.

"I wanted to d...die." She was sobbing. "I just wanted it to end. He wouldn't stop. I couldn't escape, and he said if I told anyone, something really bad would happen to them. I was so afraid I would have a baby, and then everyone would know what a dirty, filthy girl I was. I couldn't bear that. He told me if I let him do those things to me, that he wouldn't do it to anyone else. That I would be saving other little girls."

"You sacrificed yourself to save others. You endured this evil so no one else would have to, even though we know he lied. There is no greater love, than someone who lays down his or her own life for another. You didn't know that high law then, but now you do. Well done my, Melissa." He looked at the cupboard over the top of the refrigerator. "What happened, Beloved?" He asked again.

"I wanted to die. I just wanted to escape. I knew Mummy had medicines in this cupboard. No one was home, except me."

"Open the cupboard." Time Weaver instructed her. "And show me."

Reaching up, she slowly opened the door. There, in precisely the same place it had been, all those many years before, was that bottle. Haltingly, carefully, she reached into the cupboard and took the bottle.

Pleadingly, she silently begged Time Weaver. What for, she didn't actually understand. Looking at the bottle in her hand, she read the label again *'Caution, do not take. May cause death or blindness.'*

Slowly, slowly, she took the lid off the bottle. Time Weaver held his hand out for it. Willingly she put it gently in his hand.

He looked at her. All the love in the universe in that one look. Every part of her mind, emotions, and body flooded with love from that one look.

And then he drank her poison.

Shock.

Speechless silence.

Heavy, silver silence.

Silence poised on that moment, in that act. Her whole life in the juncture of his deed.

Her hand flew to grab at the bottle even as she realised the futility of it, the deed already accomplished.

"No! No! No, no, no." Horrified expression of disbelief. "That was for me, not you."

Engulfing sobs wracked her as she sank as a puddle, onto the ground. "It was for me," she repeated. "It was for me! You shouldn't have done that."

Time Weaver crouched down beside her, the empty poison bottle still in his hand. "I did it for you, Melissa.

I drank the poison so you wouldn't have to. But it's all for nothing, without me in the centre of your life, Melissa."

Looking at him through red puffy eyes, an ache of guilt and no way of rectitude.

"Who are you? Why have you done this?"

He ignored her questions, standing up instead. She watched him.

The insubstantial place started changing.

As though a scene changed in a movie, thousands of Angels appeared, some carrying the most costly clothing she could ever dream of. A robe was pulled over his head by two angels who bowed respectfully and backed away, worshipping him as they left. Another Angel appeared, carrying a circlet of gold, which was fastened around his throat. Two more Angels came with a cloak whose hem was festooned with stars. The stars themselves had life, and the cloak was woven from a rainbow. Gabriel came and placed a sceptre, named righteousness, in his right hand. And yet another Angel brought Him sandals for His feet, and under those feet was the entirety of galaxies and universes, the earth, the sun, and the moon. All that was known and unknown to mankind.

All present bowed low as the shimmering figure of a man walked toward Time Weaver. She could not see him clearly, for his face was covered in such brightness. There was a cloud of holiness about the man, and He spoke saying, "This is my beloved Son, in whom I am well pleased." The man placed a crown of such beauty on Time Weaver's head. It had no rival of anything that Melissa had ever seen.

The awe and reverence of all the Angels present, filled the space, and the space seemed to increase without end. Melissa involuntarily stepped back. She looked down, for a feeling of shame hovered in her heart.

In front of her, appeared a crystal mirror, where she saw her reflection.

Even as she looked, layer after layer was falling off her. Each layer named pride, rebellion, anger, hatred, jealousy, uncleanness. So many layers, so much sin. They fell onto the ground, where they were seen for what they were, an insubstantial barrier of lies. Her life was naked and uncovered. Everything she had hidden behind, now lay exposed.

Two Angels walked over to her. One had a sash across his garment, and on it was written, 'Understanding.' The other Angel waited respectfully, while Understanding pierced Melissa's mind with a sword. Sudden clarity pushed aside the cobwebs of self-deception, and in that instant, Wisdom cried out, "My daughter, if you accept my words and store up my commands within you, turning your ear to Wisdom, and applying your heart to Understanding, indeed, if you call out for insight and cry aloud for Understanding, and if you look for it as for silver, and search for it as for hidden treasure, then you will understand the fear of the Lord, and find the knowledge of God."

There was a sliding feeling as Deception slithered off her mind, taking his hands from across her eyes.

In the barrenness of her life, in that infinitesimal moment of lucidity, she saw.

Jesus stood before her, and His name of Time Weaver was woven into His crown. "Choose," He said, "Choose this day, whom you will serve. Be it yourself or be it me. But choose."

Flashing across the screen of her mind, was all she had been shown. The courtroom scene, where mankind had given their destiny into the hand of the evil one. Time Weaver stating that He would be the sacrificial Lamb, and then that horrifying whipping, that even now, she could not fully recall to mind, for her mind refused to remember it all. Finally, she saw him, where he had taken all her stuff, all the things that the world threw at him, everything that Ken and Grandpop had done to her, were done to Him.

He held out to her the empty poison bottle. "Everything I did, I did for you, Melissa, but remember the hole in the tapestry. Only you can choose. I will not force you. If you choose to follow me, then it is an act of your free will. You have lived your life without me. If you continue to live like this, then after you enter eternity, there is no going back. It will be an eternity without me. Darkness will consume you."

She was bewildered for a moment, and said, "But where could I go without you? You have spoken words of life to me and given me understanding. I know now that you are the Jesus that Amy speaks of." Looking down at her hands that were twisting and interlacing in agitation, she whispered, "I didn't understand at first what I was seeing. And I suppose I will never really be able to fully comprehend what you did. But then I saw you willingly allowing those evil things to be done to you, when I saw that you took all the filth on you, that had been done to me, and you didn't have to. But you did it anyway."

Her breath was coming in panting gasps, as she finally spoke out, "When I saw that, how could I not love you? But when you drank my poison...." gulping choking cries. "When you drank that. You did that, so I didn't have to. You took my suicide." A keening wail broke out of her. "You did that for me, and I've done nothing, except to deny you exist and live in my own selfishness."

He stepped towards her. She looked up at him, in his radiance, beauty and majesty surrounding him, and held out her hand to him. "I believe," is all she said.

"Then I have something for you," and he held out something folded, but it shimmered with light and reflected back the glory that encircled him.

"What is it?" she asked curiously. It was so beautiful. She reached out to touch it and felt the life pulsating from it. Most curious.

He smiled and beckoned to one of the Angels, who brought over a loom. Carefully, taking the shimmering fabric, he stretched it over the loom.

"OH! It's my tapestry!" She looked from the tapestry to Time Weaver. "It's changed!"

"Yes, it's changed. I promised you, if you gave me centre place, that the tapestry of your life would change, and so it has."

Where the muddy, muted colours had run into the despair of her life, and where the hole in the middle of the tapestry had been, was a picture that told of where despair had taken over. It was now a thing of hope and beauty. The deadness surrounding the dull and confused part had somehow changed. The colours were still there, but they seemed to have been given life. She could see the small roots of sapling trees growing in the muddy portion, and new growth pushing its way through into the future. Trees reaching for the, as yet, unwoven tapestry of her life. She could see seeds buried in the dirt, just beginning to sprout.

Where the hole had been, there was a weave of such glory, that she could not take it all in with one glance. Every tiny square of the tapestry cloth had an infinitesimal depth to it. A crown. Two hearts intertwined together. A new gown, glorious in its gossamer beauty of righteousness. New shoes, a light, and a lamb. She saw that ugly cross right in the centre, and surrounding where the hole had been, somehow living light shone out of it. Symbols appeared randomly scattered, but closer inspection showed a definite pattern. Each symbol represented part of her journey together with Time Weaver. But the most stunning part of all lay in the muddy, muted hues directly under where that barbaric cross had been woven in.

On the desolation of what had been Melissa's life, the cross stood alone. Running down the rough splintered wood was a brilliant, scarlet thread, which spilled down into the mud. Each drop of blood changed the murky barrenness into vibrant, rich earth browns. Where each drop of that scarlet thread of blood touched, great red precious stones lay in plain sight for everyone to see. The glory of the tapestry was overwhelming.

"Do you see, my Melissa? I have given you the treasures of darkness, riches stored in secret places, I have taken away your sins, and now I am giving you these fine new garments." He beckoned, and two angels appeared, handing him something of great beauty. "I will clothe you in righteousness and anoint you with the oil of my love."

The angels respectfully took the garment that Time Weaver was holding, and pulled it over Melissa's head. The feeling. Oh, the wonder and joy and love that enveloped her. Peace flooded into her mind, and understanding stirred deep within. And she felt clean.

Time Weaver looked at her with such pride and joy. "There is one thing left to do."

"What is that?" she said

"Welcome you to our family. Welcome home, my beautiful child. My Father and I have been waiting for so long to adopt you as our own." He reached out and grabbed her into the biggest hug.

Angels all around them were cheering. It sounded as though a party was going on.

"They are cheering for you. Another lost soul who has found her way home."

The wildness burst its way out of her soul, with a need to dance frenetically in joy for him, for the joy was erupting out of her. Unable to resist, she took hold of Time Weaver's hands and started dancing. Each step threw up a spark of joy, or praise, or love, or laughter. She stopped looking at them after a while, and just accepted, that while she was with Time Weaver, her heart was complete.

He took her a little way distance from the party.

"It's time to go back, Melissa." His hands were cupping her face.

"No! No, I don't want to leave you. That means I have to go back and face that world. No. I don't want to. It's too hard."

"Melissa, your job on earth is not finished yet. You have many, many, to bring into freedom in me. Do you think all this has been without purpose? All you have learned? No, my sweet. You have been shown the things of Heaven so that you, too, can tell others. Your life is as a witness to my love and goodness. As you heal from the childhood trauma, others will see more and more of me in your heart. This then, is Truth."

"But what if I mess up? How will I find you again?" She reached for him desperately, so afraid to be apart from the source of her life.

Smiling wistfully, he said, "Yes, you will mess up. You will make mistakes, and you will act in rebellion.

But I am in you, and you are in me, so just come to me with a contrite heart and let my blood cleanse you again."

She nodded. "Yes. OK, I understand that. But Time Weaver, what about James?"

"His journey is his journey. Not yours." He bent down and kissed her on the forehead. "Remember, Melissa, I will never leave you nor forsake you. Don't ever take your eyes off me."

He touched her, and as she fell, the two angels caught her. He nodded to them, and they bowed respectfully to him.

Carrying Melissa so carefully between them, they stepped through the portal from one realm to the other, and very softly laid her heart and soul and spirit back into her body.

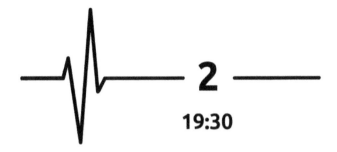

2

19:30

"Melissa, Melissa. Wake up." A disembodied voice called her. She struggled up out of the swamping dark.

"We're going to take the breathing tube out of your mouth now, ok?" Dimly, a voice reached out to her. A swirling muttering of words briefly registered, before she lapsed back into the dark place.

A hand rubbed her arm gently. "Melissa. Wake up."

The sound of shoes squeaking on a linoleum floor started to penetrate the smothering murk.

"Open your eyes, Melissa," the voice commanded her.

"Ugggh"

"Mask at 15 litres per minute, reducing down," one of the voices drifted into her consciousness.

Something unpleasant was inserted in her nostrils.

"Blood Pressure 110 over 65, Oxygen saturation coming up, 93%."

"Melissa. Melissa, open your eyes, Melissa."

In between a groan and a sigh, she surfaced from the depths back to consciousness.

"Open your eyes, Melissa." And she blinked in the harsh light that startled her eyes awake.

"Blood Pressure normal 110 over 70, oxygen saturation 97%."

"Squeeze my hand, Melissa," a voice commanded her.

"Time Weaver?" she croaked.

"The time is 7.30 pm. You have been unconscious for 25 hours. Do you remember what happened, Melissa?" A man was standing by her, asking her questions.

Her brain didn't want to respond. Everything wanted to go back to sleep.

"Melissa, do you remember what happened?" The man asked her again.

Blinking against the light, blinking off the sleep tendrils, she looked at where the voice was coming from. Something she had to remember. Something, fading fast. Reaching back into the darkness of sleep for it. Someone. What was it?

"Do you know the time, Melissa?" the man asked her.

Time! Time Weaver. Remember Time Weaver.

"Oh, you're back. Good." A man was bending over her, smiling. "Right, team. Good work. She will remain in ICU for the rest of the night, and we'll reassess in the morning. Meanwhile, there is an anxious husband waiting outside."

A multitude of people left, and James came in.

"Oh, thank God! I thought I had lost you!" he exclaimed, as he started crying.

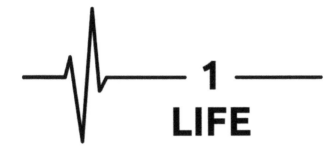

1
LIFE

James had gone back to work, and the children were back at school. Melissa was alone for the first time in a week, since coming home.

There had been many words spoken. A lot of healing between her and James. Regular appointments scheduled with Psych Services, and strategies put in place if she ever felt that black hole beckon her again. Her meds made her feel woozy, but as her body adjusted to them, the nauseous feeling lessened every day.

Taking her coffee and the Bible Amy had given her, she went outside to sit in the sun in the garden. Oscar followed along behind her, plaintively telling everyone that he had never been fed in his life. "Oh, Oscar, puss. You little fatty. Don't tell lies."

She held her face up to the sun, closing her eyes and basking in the warmth.

She was alive. Peace and serenity as she had never felt before, surrounded her. The only words she could find to explain this, was that her struggle was now overlain with hope, like the colours of Spring, of new life; the colour of a tree bursting into leaf intermingled with anticipation.

Using her foot, she pushed out another of the garden chairs and murmured, "Time Weaver, come and sit with me, while I read."

She opened the Bible randomly and started to read.

> *'I saw the Lord always before me.*
> *Because He is at my right hand,*
> *I will not be shaken.*
> *Therefore, my heart is glad,*
> *and my tongue rejoices,*
> *My body also will rest in hope because you*
> *will not abandon me to the realm of the dead.*
> *You will not let your holy one see decay.*
> *You have made known to me*
> *the paths of life;*
> *You will fill me with joy in your presence.'*

Giggling, she said, "I know you are here. I can't see you, but I know you are here, Time Weaver. It is only as I see myself reflected in you, that my foundations will come into right alignment."

1

And the still small voice
echoed in her mind,
Remember, Melissa, I will never leave you.
Don't take your eyes off me.

Justine's
Story

The story you have read about Melissa and James is somewhat my story. The sole difference is that even though I was suicidal for 45 years, my inner strength and religious belief system stopped me from carrying it through.

The scenes you read with Melissa, Grandpop and Ken is my story. The deliverance from suicide is Jesus. That is exactly what happened as He walked me back through that horror. Even now, reliving watching Him drink my poison, is enough to force me to my knees in adoration.

oooooo OOO oooooo

Living as an abuse victim is extremely difficult. Living *with* an abuse victim is also difficult. Their whole response to life is coloured by the lens of their experiences, distorted in great pain.

The change comes, when the victim becomes a survivor.

I was 34 before I finally faced up to the damage that kept me as a victim. That night is etched on the screen of my mind. I asked my father to come over because I was going to tell him what had happened.

But the words stuck in my throat. I froze. Panic reached hands out from my belly and kept pulling the words back down. Finally, Dad said that it was getting late, and he had to leave.

Forcing my mouth to cooperate with my mind, the words startled out of my mouth. "Ken and Grandpop did this," and told him the story of what they did.

No parent ever wants to hear that, for it means that they failed to keep their child safe. My poor father went grey. I remember. I remember that I dumped my pain on him, and held him responsible for what happened.

And then the anger with overwhelming rage started to manifest in such storms, that I felt wildly out of control.

Being brought up with a church background, I had felt it was not Godly, nor Christ-like to feel such anger. I forced it back down. Stuffed it back into my mind and emotions. Repented constantly, for the utter hatred towards the two men who completely destroyed the innocence of little me.

Without understanding why, I fought the violent rage inside me, all the while thinking, *'I shouldn't be angry.'* So many false assumptions and beliefs that crippled me and brought me crashing into depression. If only someone had told me years ago that I was allowed to be angry about what happened to me, it would have relieved a whole lot of internal anger, the anger of complete helplessness.

But Jesus was extremely angry at times, and he gave vent to that anger. But the difference was this. I vented my anger all over everyone. My husband, my children, my father, my friends. What I didn't understand about the anger I was feeling, was that it was righteous anger against injustice.

Weight issues started to emerge. When I was 16, Ken told me that if I lost weight, I could be a model. What did that tell me? That I was fat. Looking back at my teenage photos, I was anything but fat, but the distortion in my mind of my self-image told me a different story. So, when I started to confront the abuse, these words came back, and I started comfort eating.

Life turned into a time of bitter control. For with abuse, a victim can only feel safe when they can control their environment.

Control freak. Manipulation. Every aspect of my life had to be controlled, and that included my husband and children. If something felt out of control, and I couldn't keep it within my grasp, I would fly into a rage. My parameters were not safe.

Finally, Stan told me that in order to keep the children safe, he would have to leave and take them away, unless I got help.

For two years, I sought counselling with a trained psychologist. Unfortunately, the prevailing thinking at the time was to empower the victim to ensure they would never be victimised again. All I did was to swap the victim mentality for one of bitterness. Men were to be despised. And that included my husband.

The potency of the effect of abuse, is life-long. It is a life sentence. The impact flows over into every aspect of life, work, marriage, children, friends, church. All relationships suffer, for they are perverted by trust issues.

The child who is trapped inside, rages to be let out, to be understood and listened to. The trauma that is still retained at even a very basic level, carries with it fear and terror. Fear and terror run with anger, and after a period of time, burst out of their hiding place, manifesting in physical illnesses and depression.

I had been prayed for, I had rebuked and declared. I had ignored and cried. Nothing worked. The pain remained. The festering wounds of the abuse erupted frequently, and my husband wore it all like a garment I constantly threw over him, until he could no longer stay around me.

There was only one way through my trauma. One way to salvage my marriage and one way to get free - Jesus.

Don't get me wrong. Jesus had been in my life always. But this was a deeper level. A far different type of love story - just Him and I.

Our time together was driving to and from work. I was alone in the car; no interruptions and He had my full attention. For some reason, He never called me by name, for our relationship is that of intimacy. We are known to each other. He only spoke, and I knew He was there. I can still see the place where I was when He spoke that time.

"I want you to forgive Ken and Grandpop."

My reaction was less than gracious and loving. I won't write the words I yelled; except they were along the lines of 'You have got to *beep* be kidding. I want them to *beep* rot in hell. *beep beep beep.*'

We tussled for weeks. Every day He asked me the same question, and every day He got the same response. Until one day, He said, "I want you to be willing to be made willing to forgive."

I considered that all the way to work. I pondered that all the way home. I knew what the Bible said in Matthew 6:14, 'If you forgive those who sin against you, your heavenly Father will forgive you.' I understood the ramifications of refusing to forgive. I also realized that forgiveness was not for Ken and Grandpop's benefit, it was to set *me* free. Finally, I said, "OK. Yes, Lord. I will allow you that. I am willing to be made willing to forgive them."

For six months, back and forth, driving the same road, arguing the same thing, my heart gradually softened, until I finally got to the place where I could say, 'OK, I'm willing to forgive, but it will have to be your forgiveness, Jesus, because I still don't actually forgive.' And that was all He needed. A few years later, I saw my cousin at a family gathering, and even though I was shaking inside, I went up to him and put my arms around him and said, "Ken, I forgive you." And to my surprise. I did. The Lord had worked in my mind and my heart to such an extent, that I really did forgive him.

During all this time period, my marriage had continued to deteriorate, until it was no longer tenable. Neither of us could live in this hell-hole, created by a broken little girl and a man who could no longer deal with all this junk. We were at breaking point and for a period were estranged, although forced by financial constraints, were still living under the same roof.

Driving again, back and forth, to and from work, I cried out to the Lord, "LORD! I've done everything I know to do. I have said 'I love you,' trusting you to make the words a reality. I've cooked the nice meals, tried to be all that he needs, but nothing is working. We are both too broken."

Jesus just listened to me and then He said, "Who told you to do all that?"

"What?"

He repeated, "Who told you to do all that?"

I spluttered, "What?" Again, He asked. "What Lord? What do you mean? I thought that's what I should be doing, what I had to do."

"I didn't tell you to do that." He paused a moment and then said, "All I told you to do, is to *just be.*"

Now I was really confused. "What do you mean?"

I love Jesus, He's so patient. He said, "What are you doing right now?"

"Well, I'm driving, Lord."

"Yes, you are driving, but what are you doing to drive?"

I do wonder about anyone who passed by me during this time, for my facial expressions would have been hilarious. "Um, well, I'm steering the car, and my foot is on the accelerator."

"Good," He said, "Now, HOW are you making the car go?"

"I'm not? The engine is. I'm just sitting here?"

"EXCELLENT!" He said. "And what are you doing to hold yourself up, while you are driving the car?"

"Well nothing, the seat is holding me up. I'm just sitting and ...... OH! I'm just 'being.' I'm not doing anything to hold myself up or to propel the car along."

The light came on. *Just be,* He had said. Stop striving. Stop all your good works. Stop trying to fix everything. *Just be* and rest in Him. Incredibly, within a few months, Stan and I had fallen in love again.

We still had a long way to go to overcoming the abuse issues, and the damage in me, but Jesus had our feet on the right path. My lack of trust in anyone, along with my determination not to allow anyone to get the better of me, had manifested into our marriage, causing a lot of friction. We had to deal with that. It came down to a choice. I had to choose to trust Stan and allow myself to become vulnerable to him. Over time, the trust was extended to a few people whom I grew to understand, did actually love me, and there were no ulterior motives. That, in wanting to know me, they didn't want anything from me, except my friendship and love.

Trust grew.

It was the suicide that was the last nail in the coffin. Jesus led me back through time, back to when I was 12 and desperate to die. He took me into my mother's kitchen again. Jesus was standing right by me, by the cupboard when I was 12. I reached into that cupboard and took that bottle of poison, holding it in my hand, and as He stood there, I gave him the poison.

He took the bottle, opened it and drank it all, so I wouldn't have to.

I tried to grab the bottle off him, but couldn't. He had already drunk my poison.

It shook me completely. And suicide left me forever.

I became a survivor, no longer a victim.

Not everyone has the same experiences. We all receive healing in different ways, but the basis, the foundation of it all, is the same. A willingness to let go of the blame, and to allow God to perform open-heart surgery on us. It is extremely painful.

As a few more years rolled by, the lessons I had been taught, were taught again and again, over and over, until they were deeply embedded in me.

I had one more lesson to learn.

My beloved Stan had a heart attack. The paramedics got him to the emergency room, where his heart stopped. My daughter pushed me out of the room, where I stood helplessly on the other side of the wall, listening to calls of *'paddles' 'adrenaline' 'again, more adrenaline, paddles again.'*

He was resuscitated and rushed to surgery, where I was allowed to go and say goodbye. I had no idea whether I would ever see him again.

Obviously, he did pull through, but the trauma stayed with me. The doctor ordered anti-anxiety drugs. I took one and looked at the side effects and threw them away. Still, I would hear an ambulance and break down. The scenes were in front of me constantly. I could not function.

And then Jesus stepped into the picture again. He came up to me. "Beloved." He said, and put one finger under my chin, tilting my head up, so I was looking full at Him. "Don't take your eyes off me. Keep looking at me."

So, what did Time Weaver say to Melissa? "Don't ever take your eyes off me."

It's the only way through.

These three main things of forgiveness, letting go of our struggle to 'just be,' and then keep your focus on Him, are the only way to healing from any abuse.

On my journey through life, I have discovered that God never wastes anything, and all the pain, the grief and terror are not for nothing. If I have gone through my pain, just to bring you this message of freedom and hope, then my life has been worth every single tear.

Through all I have gone through and will go through in the future, my Father God loves me so much, that He has extended all He had to me, and bought back my freedom at massive cost to Himself.

An abuse victim is like a twisted tree.

When a gardener plants a sapling tree, the tree is tied to a stake to hold it secure during storms, just in the same way as we care for a little one, bringing in boundaries for the child's security. If, as the tree grows, the gardener does not loosen the ties and remove the stake, the tree will eventually grow to embrace the ties and stake, and it becomes part of the tree. If the gardener then tries to remove the stake, it would kill the tree.

Children go through growth stages; physical, emotional and mental. When a child is abused, whichever emotional growth stage that child is at, when the abuse starts, this emotional stage begins to grow twisted, just like the tree.

I have screamed at God before - "WHY don't you just heal me!" I'm so glad that He is very patient and loving. It seemed to me He said (once I started listening), that if He did just reach down and do an instant healing, that we would be like the tree where, if the gardener removed the stake; it would cripple us completely, for who we are today, is because of that stake. Where we were once twisted and gnarled, we are now a beautiful orchestra singing His praises.

He is offering this same freedom to all of us, whether we know Him as Abba Father, or not. His love for us surpasses anything we can conceive. It is in this love that we find answers and healing.

As we surrender our pain, our brokenness and our lives to God, through our Lord Jesus Christ, I have every confidence that He will not abandon any of us, He will not ignore us. Father will not use us as others have. He is gentle, He does not lie, and He does not manipulate.

It is only as we see ourselves reflected in Jesus, that our foundations will come into right alignment.

Jesus, I see you as in a mirror;

As you are, so am I.

Victory

Last Word

As I have been writing this book, I have been thinking about the #MeToo movement.

It struck me that with all the press and media coverage on the #MeToo, that there actually hasn't been very much solidarity amongst the Me Too group. We need each other so much.

Has there just been a lot of noise made, and then a few have used the noise to make traction for their own causes?

Has it actually sucked desperately hurting people into its vortex, and then they've been abused all over again, because they have been trying to find ANYONE who really understands and will listen, but no one really has?

Or has it really made it real how differently women are treated and how we as women often feel scared?

Is #Metoo just another five-minute trend where people like the idea, but no one is willing to make it a permanent mindset shift?

I think there has been a chance to share painful stories, to talk and share, which helps bring healing, bring things into the light.

Secrets keep us lost in the darkness, so the movement did achieve something in assisting the hurting to tentatively put their hands up to say, 'me too.'

But I feel there has been a lot of bleating noise, which created a collective energetic movement, but only as a band-aid.

How shall we change it?

VICTORY – LAST WORD

People think that intimacy is about sex.
But intimacy is about truth.
When you realise you can tell someone your truth,
When you can show yourself to them,
When you stand in front of them bare,
and their response is
"You're safe with me"
- that's intimacy

Taylor Jenkins

(from The Seven Husbands of Evelyn Hugo)

Permission requested to use the quotation.

"LOVE WAS THE MOST DIFFICULT
CHOICE FOR ME TO MAKE,
BUT NOW I HAVE EXHAUSTED
ALL OTHER OPTIONS.
MY HURT BECOMES HOPE."

Anita Mary (2012)

Author of 'Blood on the Mirror'

VICTORY – LAST WORD

"God, where can I hide from you?
You know what happened,
you know all my grief and my pain.
For all that I have gone through, for all the shame,
you have promised me a new life, a new garment,
a spirit of praise for the heaviness of mourning.
In Jesus' name, God, I ask that you set me free,
that you will walk with me and you will never let me go,
and I know you will not hurt me.
Guide me through this healing, show me your love.
That I might know you!
That I might know and experience Jesus,
all because of what Jesus did for me."

Rejoice, for your name is written in heaven.
Luke 10: 20b, NIV

…to him who overcomes, I will give a white stone
with a new name written on it,
known only to him who receives it.
Revelation 2:17b   NIV

… He breathed His breath (His *own* breath) into man's nostrils, and the man became a living being.

Genesis 2:7 NIV

There is a time for everything and a season for every activity under heaven:

to be born and to die, to plant and to uproot, to kill and to heal, to tear down and to build, to weep and to laugh, to mourn and to dance.

Ecclesiastes 3:1 – 4   NIV

We know that in all things, God works for the good of those who love Him; who have been called according to His purpose. For those God foreknew, He also predestined to be conformed to the likeness of His Son.

Romans 8:28, 29   NIV

Do not throw away your confidence;

it will be richly rewarded.

You need to persevere

so that when you have done the will of God,

you will receive what He has promised.

Hebrews 10:35 – 36 NIV

And this is the confidence that we have in him that,

if we ask anything according to his will, he hears us.

1 John 5:14 KJV

APPENDIX

The following are excerpts from the book, with Scripture references to back them up.

Page 75

"There is a saying in the sacred annals of Heaven - if anyone causes one of these little ones to stumble, it would be better for them to have a large millstone hung around their neck and to be drowned in the depths of the sea."

Matthew 18:6

Page 84

"Melissa, I am not a man that I would lie to you. I cannot lie. I am the Way, I am Truth, and I hold your life safely in my hands. I am Trust. You can trust me, Little One."

Adapted from Numbers 23:19

Page 95

The **laminin** molecules are named according to their chain composition.

Thus, **laminin-511** contains α5, β1, and γ1 chains. ... The trimeric proteins intersect to form a cross-like structure that can bind to other cell membrane and extracellular matrix molecules.

Laminin molecule as on Wikipedia.

Page 101

Time Weaver just waited silently, then he blew in her direction, speaking quietly, "The North Wind has awakened. Come South Wind, blow on this garden that its fragrance may spread everywhere."

Paraphrased from Song of Solomon 4:16

Page 101

Time Weaver sang over her;

Taken from Zephaniah 3:17

Page 101

Lay down in peace and sleep
I only make you to dwell in safety

Psalms 4: 8

Page 122

"The Most High God wants you to know the truth. In knowing the truth, you will be set free."

John 8:32

Page 129

"Oh, every time one of mankind cries righteous tears, they are caught and held in a crystal bottle awaiting the time for release. Precious in the sight of the Lord are their tears."

Psalms 56:8 – "You put my tears into your bottle, are they not in your book?"

Page 131

"A rooster crowed. She looked around her and saw a group. Soldiers. Guarding a prisoner."

Luke 22:55 - 62

Page 135

"Even as the flagellum broke open and even as it destroyed, a song was released. *By these stripes you are healed.*"

Isaiah 53:5

Page 154

"I would crown you with a diadem to glorify and adorn you, in place of the worthlessness of your life. I will pour my oil of joy in exchange for your sorrow, so you will rejoice. You will live in praise for the rest of your life, swapping the heaviness you are carrying for my joy."

Isaiah 61:3

Page 154,155

"Did you realise that you were already in your grandmother's ovum, at the time of her birth? And that she passed that same DNA onto your mother, who then passed it onto you? That at the time of your conception, the DNA you had present in your own ovum, was also going to pass onto Alex, and then again onto Alex's daughter?"

mtDNA is transmitted through the female egg. The mtDNA found in the egg is nonrecombinant, meaning that it does not combine with any other

DNA so that it is passed down virtually unchanged through the direct maternal line over the generations. You inherited your mtDNA exclusively from your mother.

https://phillipsdnaproject.com/faq-sections/144-mitochondrial-dna-explained

Page 158

"You sacrificed yourself to save others." Time Weaver poured those loving eyes all over her. "There is no greater love, than someone who lays down their own life for another. Well done, my Melissa."

John 15:13

Page 160

And yet another Angel brought Him sandals for His feet, and under those feet was the entirety of galaxies and universes, the earth, the sun and moon. All that was known and unknown to mankind.

Isaiah 66:1; Acts 7:49; Hebrews 2:8

Page 161

There was a cloud of holiness about the man, and He spoke saying, "This is my beloved Son in whom I am well pleased."

Matthew 17:5; Mark 9:7; Luke 9:35

Page 161

Understanding pierced Melissa's mind with a sword. Sudden clarity pushed aside the cobwebs of self-deception, and in that instant, Wisdom cried out...

Proverbs 1:2; Proverbs 1:20

Page 162

Wisdom cried out, "My daughter, if you accept my words and store up my commands within you, turning your ear to Wisdom, and applying your heart to Understanding, indeed, if you call out for insight and cry aloud for Understanding, and if you look for it as for silver, and search for it as for hidden treasure, then you will understand the fear of the Lord, and find the knowledge of God."

Proverbs 2:3 – 5

Page 162

"Choose." He said. "Choose this day, whom you will serve. Be it yourself or be it me. But choose."

Joshua 24:15

Page 163

She was bewildered for a moment, and said, "But where could I go without you? You have spoken words of life to me and given me understanding. I know now that you are the Jesus that Amy speaks of."

Psalm 139:7,8; John 6:67

Page 166

"Do you see, my Melissa? I have given you the treasures of darkness, riches stored in secret places,"

Isaiah 45:3

Page 166

"See, I have taken away your sins, and now I am giving you these fine new garments."

Zechariah 3:4

Page 166

"They are cheering for you. Another lost soul who has found her way home."

Luke 15:10

Page 174

'I saw the Lord always before me.
Because He is at my right hand,
I will not be shaken.
Therefore, my heart is glad, and my tongue
rejoices, my body also will rest in hope because
you will not abandon me
to the realm of the dead.
You will not let your holy one see decay.
You have made known to me
the paths of life;
You will fill me with joy in your presence.'

Psalm 16:10; Acts 2:25 - 28

Page 179

Jesus was extremely angry at times, and he gave vent to that anger.

Matthew 21

ABOUT THE AUTHOR

Jesus has always been the centre of all that Justine is, and she has known the Lord from a young age.

Justine is a revelatory, prophetic writer, who is passionate to see the Church in her rightful place in Christ. With a lifetime of knowing the Lord, her inner strength and understanding of the things of God, shows in her daily interactions with others.

Justine and her husband of 39 years, Stan, live in Auckland, New Zealand, with their two crazy cats. They have two lovely adult daughters.

Have you read "In the Beginning - I Am Beryl" Book One (2018)? If not, it's a must-read!

This is the first book in a 5-book chronology taking you through the Biblical accounts from the perspective of the Beryl Stone, mentioned 8 times in the Bible, from before time to John's Revelation of the end of time.

If you've read "In the Beginning - I Am Beryl," you will not want to miss the next in the series, "A Stone in My Sandal - I Am Beryl" Book Two! Pre-order from Justine Orme now!

Email theauthorJustine@gmail.com

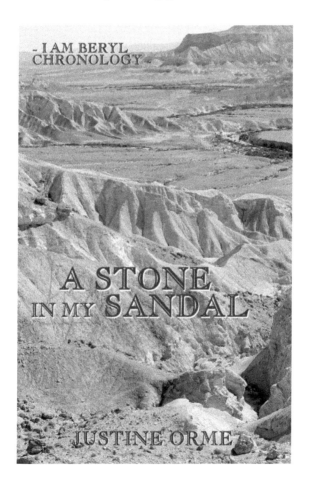

If you have been impacted by this book, and would like to talk to, or write Justine about it,

Email her at theauthorJustine@gmail.com

Or you can also follow Justine on Facebook:

www.facebook.com/theauthorJustine

and on Instagram:

www.instagram.com/justineorme

Lightning Source UK Ltd.
Milton Keynes UK
UKHW011159190822
407505UK00001B/282